MANDY

WHEELER

A FOUR FATHERS STORY

KER DUKEY

I am dark. Calculating. A single father.

I have secrets that would horrify most people.
Stalking is a habit I refuse to break—and what happens
after is a sweet reward.
My life is exactly the way I have designed it.
But an undeserving, sick monster is dating my only
daughter.
Until I deal with my problem, I can't truly enjoy
everything I've created.

My name is Jax Wheeler.

I'm a twisted, evil, insane man.
People may be afraid of me,
but it doesn't stop them from wanting me.

Author Note

This novel is DARK suspense.

It may contain triggers for the sensitive reader.

It's also part of a series, if you haven't checked out

the other books in this awesome series, but intend to,

PLEASE read the prior books before starting Wheeler,

as it contains HUGE spoilers and will ruin the other

titles for you.

Other than that enjoy the journey.

DEDICATION

For all my

FUCKED UP

readers.

Life would be boring without a few psychopaths

to shake things up.

PROLOGUE

J A X

Psychopath red flag
#**1**
They create a façade

Six years ago...

THE BOISTEROUS LAUGHTER AND CONSTANT catcalls anytime a woman walks past the Pearson boys irritates me on a level I'm not used to.

These people are mundane and my intellect is dropping points every second I'm forced to be around them.

Overcooked, chargrilled chicken is dumped on my paper plate by Rowan, my twelve-year-old firecracker. She beams up at me, and I can't help but relax my tense posture and offer her a smile in return.

"Thank you," I tell her, picking up the flesh and taking a chunk into my mouth. I chew and swallow to appease her, but it's rubbery and lodges in my trachea, more than likely because Eric insists on barbecuing his own meat at these get-togethers rather than hiring a cook or caterers. For someone who's rich and likes to flaunt it, the paper plates he has us all juggling are cheap. Just like half the women here. Not hiring a chef to barbeque is an alpha male trait, and he's too busy drooling over the half-dressed housewives flaunting their bought tits and veneer smiles to concentrate on doing a good job of it.

"I'm going to get my suit and swim with the boys," Rowan tells me, pulling my attention back to her. She's been a friend of the Pearson boys since we moved here six months ago.

They attend the same school, kids' parties, after school activities. I can't escape the little bastards.

I don't like her being around four boys, especially

Eric Pearson's boys. Those kids are trouble. Hayden is the oldest, but he isn't right in the head. I don't like the way his eyes track my daughter—as though he might do something to her. Over my fucking dead body. Brock, the second to oldest, and around the same age as Rowan, is destined to turn out just like his dad, even has the same goddamn smirk. Nixon is a few years younger than Rowan, but seems lost inside his head and is always muttering under his breath—something I can certainly relate to. And the youngest, Camden, is still a titty-baby momma's boy despite being in third or fourth grade. Eventually, Eric Pearson will influence that kid too. His idea of role modeling is cheating on his wife and throwing money at any problems that arise. The Pearson boys don't stand a chance of being anything other than scum. It's in their gene pool.

But Rowan sees the best in everyone, which works for me, so I don't try to dull that glitter from her personality. Her soft brown hair that matches mine fans over her delicate shoulders, and her eyelids flutter as she waits for my permission.

I scan the boys who are all taking turns dive bombing into the swimming pool, and visions of the water turning red as I wade through with a carving knife and cut each pecker from their pubescent bodies invade my mind, bringing a real smile to my lips.

Apparently, it's healthy to socialize with your neighbors, and good for Rowan to have play dates. Those play dates didn't used to include boys and swimsuits, though.

This is going to be a real test of restraint.

"Go ahead, sweetheart." I nod my head in the direction of our house.

Her auburn hair falls down her back and sways as she bounces across the lawn and out of the gate.

I pull on the collar of the shirt I took ten minutes choosing just to come to this shit-show. I hate wearing polo shirts, but it's what I see most men wear when they're going for a casual look. I paired it with some beige slacks, but I'm thinking I should have gone for shorts like everyone else here. It's hard for me sometimes to fit in— to adjust to the norm and blend in with other parents.

Bodies mingle and talk animatedly to each other, and all I want to do is flee back to the comfort of my own house—my own company. I have things to do, people to check up on. One of Eric's wife's friends keeps looking over at me offering a coy smile, but she's older than the girls I like and too fake. I hate the rich women who think paying to have toxins pumped into their skin makes them look young and attractive.

They're wrong.

It makes them look swollen and desperate. Grow old gracefully or die young, but freezing your youth in time forever is simply pathetic.

Eric catches my eye and summons me over with a motion of his hand, the muscles in his abdomen flexing, showing he works out.

In only a pair of shorts, his over-tanned skin is cooking under the summer sun, and I think about the damage that would show under a black light.

Vanity is such an ugly trait in humans, and Eric has it in abundance. I debate not going over. Who the hell is he to beckon me? But for Rowan, I will make the effort, play the part, wear the façade.

"Eric," I say with a tilt of my head. I have the brief urge to grab his head and plant it on the grill he's tossing steaks on, smelling the burning of his flesh, relishing the screams and sizzle. The feeling washes over me like a red mist, dimming the sounds around me and making my fingers twitch, but it drifts away with the smoke of the barbeque evaporating.

"Jaxson, glad you could make it," he says. Calling me "Jaxson" is another sign of power. He knows I go by Jax. I've corrected him many times in the past. I think it's because his wife, Julia, calls me Jax. She's over familiar with me whenever an occasion arises where we have to talk, her hands are touchy feely, and it makes my skin crawl so he likes to put me in my place.

Desperation is also a trait in people I despise. But it's amusing he finds me threatening.

"This is Trevor and Levi. They work with me." He introduces me to his partners, undermining their positions—another show of how badly he needs to be the dominant alpha, while emphasizing his lack of respect for anyone around him. Unbeknownst to him, I already know exactly who they are. I did my research about Eric before buying the property next door. He's the CEO of Four Fathers Freight. Levi Kingston is a partner, along with Trevor Blackstone and Mateo Bonilla. FFF is a U.S. based global packaging company and delivery service founded in 2005 by Eric and his partners. They're a rapidly growing business and already the third largest transport company operator in the U.S. Total revenue for last year hit over forty billion. This is why Eric is such a cocky sonofabitch. Money does strange things to the simple-minded.

I offer a polite hello and study each of them. Trevor appears more reserved than Eric and Levi, who both tip their beers to their lips and eyeball a girl barely into her teens as she saunters past and jumps on the back of Hayden, Eric's oldest son. She makes a screeching sound when he jumps with her into the pool. The splash soaks a couple younger children, making them cry. Her bikini top lifts as she crashes into the water, her young tits on display for a brief moment. I look away, uninterested in child nudity.

"They grow up so fast." Eric grins, and Levi smirks in return. "Amen to that, brother."

Perverts. I'm all for looking at a beautiful woman, but teens who barely have fluff on their cunts do nothing for me, and men who prey on them make my blood heat.

Levi is so much like Eric, they could have been spat out by the same mother.

I eye Levi's impeccable suit, crinkle free, his tie firmly

in place, like he's going to a wedding and not sitting in the yard of his friend in blistering heat. He sees me looking at him and narrows his eyes.

"I came straight from the office," he barks at me, offended by my assessment of his attire.

If it were just us two and he spoke to me with such a bite, I'd remove his tongue, cook it, and feed it to Eric's wife's best friend Mona Marvel's Chihuahua she keeps in a fucking handbag over her shoulder.

"What line of work are you in, Jaxson?" Trevor asks, feigning interest and drawing my attention from imagining his friend's bloody demise.

"It's just Jax, and pharmaceuticals," I reply without elaborating. Most people assume I'm a salesman, but it's my company. It's small, but keeps Rowan and me wealthy, and sees to other needs I have.

Dark, depraved needs.

Needs that aren't appropriate to discuss over a neighborhood cookout.

He takes his time studying me, and I wonder if he sees something inside me others don't. I read he was homeless at one point. It's incredible what he's accomplished, from rags to riches, yet he still dresses like a homeless man. He should take some pride in his appearance.

"Look at the ass on Jenny Taylor. Now that's great work." Eric drools as Levi and Trevor both cast their eyes in the direction he's staring. Their other partner, Mateo, is the only decent one in the bunch and only has eyes for his wife clutched tight in his arms. Rowan has been invited to sleepovers with Mateo's daughter, Karelma, in the past, which I've allowed because I don't have to worry about him like I do his shitty, scumbag partners.

"How much do you think it cost her?" Eric muses aloud.

Trevor starts mumbling numbers as though he's actually calculating the cost of Jenny's plastic surgery. Her ass looks ridiculous. She shouldn't have paid shit for it. It's clearly a botched job and doesn't match her slender frame. Nobody pays for an ass that big. If I jabbed a knife into her ass cheek, she would leak and deflate. It's laughable what these men find attractive. She's also a mother of three and her husband plays golf with Eric. Their disloyalty says a lot about their character.

"Oh, shit. Incoming," Levi sniggers behind his beer bottle, tipping it up and taking a hearty swig.

Eric's wife Julia approaches us with fire in her eyes, and I sense a scene about to erupt. I don't want all eyes cast in my direction, and being this close to Eric when his wife is storming toward him is exactly what's going to happen. I excuse myself and slip away into the background.

The shadows offer me solace from having to speak to anyone else. I can watch Rowan, who's returned in her pink one-piece, and is now being dunked in the pool by Brock. She giggles and splashes. My daughter is growing up so fast—too fast. Her body is changing, and boys are noticing. If I could set the world alight and just live amongst the ashes, she and I forever, I would. But the world is a complicated place, and I've had to adapt and learn as I go. She was a surprise baby, one I never ever thought I'd want, but she's the only thing I've ever loved. Her happiness is why I live amongst people and not isolated in the mountains.

Before her, there was no light, no sun, just darkness. My soul was as frozen as the winter snow, silent and cold.

Deadly to anyone trapped within it.

A screech from Julia gains the attention of everyone, including the boys and Rowan. What an embarrassment, causing a scene in front of all the guests they insisted on coming over.

"You're a disgusting sonofabitch, and I'm done, Eric. I'm fucking done," Julia screams, tears rolling down her red, blotchy face, creating black streaks from her mascara.

"Calm the hell down. We have guests," Eric growls, grabbing her arms and pushing her inside the house.

Levi sniggers, and Trevor shakes his head in

disapproval. Nixon, another of Eric's offspring, exits the pool and watches his parents through the pane of glass separating them from the rest of us.

"Nix, they'll be fine, buddy," Trevor tells him as he walks over to the boy. "Grab the football and I'll kick it around with you." It's actually interesting to see them side by side. If I didn't know Eric was his father, I'd swear Trevor's DNA runs through the veins of that kid. They look identical, even down to the way they walk. It's uncanny. I wonder if Eric sees it too and questions the paternity.

Julia, you bad girl.

I check my watch and decide I'll give Rowan fifteen more minutes, then it's home and bed for her. I've fulfilled my duty. Dinner and a show. Never a dull moment in the Pearson household.

———

Tucking Rowan into bed, I can't help but sweep a

stray hair from her eyes and admire how sweet this kid is. It'll be hell keeping her safe from hormonal boys in the coming years. Luckily, I have ways.

I pick up her clothes left in a pile on her carpet and place them on the chair in the corner of her room. She grabs the picture on her bedside table with the word *Mom* emblazoned in messy letters painted across the frame and kisses it.

"Goodnight, Mommy," she says to the picture, then grins at me. "Goodnight, Daddy."

"Goodnight, sweetheart."

I turn off her light and shut her bedroom door. She's caught the sun and appears exhausted from all the swimming. Tomorrow is a non-school day, and I promised her a day of daddy-daughter fun.

Being her father isn't a hardship, but trying to offer her a stable and well-rounded childhood comes with some sacrifices.

Parties, school events, and day trips being just a few.

When I get downstairs, I grab the keys for the basement, unlock the door, and take the stairs, switching on the light. Rowan knows I keep medical supplies down here and she's not allowed to ever come in here. So when I hear movement above me, followed by footfalls on the stairs, my fists clench. She's never disobeyed the rules before.

Confusion falters my movements when Julia comes down the stairs behind me and dumps a bag on the ground at my feet.

What the fuck?

"Your door was unlocked," she explains, as if that's a good enough reason for her to enter my property without knocking and roam around like she owns the damn place. My back doors are always open because it's summer and I like the sound of the crickets chirping. No one can access the back of my property, though, so I'm perplexed at how she managed it.

She appears to know my thoughts because she

continues with her explanation of her presence in my house. In my basement. In my space. "Our children made a gate between our properties so they can come and go between the two."

She means her boys made a gate for my Rowan to creep over there. Rage coils my muscles, and I find myself picking up the screwdriver I'd left out earlier and squeezing the handle in my grip.

"I'm leaving Eric," she announces, like we're friends and I'd care what she's doing. Is she waiting for me to say something? What do I say to that? Is there a rulebook somewhere I should have read for this situation? Are we friends?

I hate this part of pretending to be like *them*.

Normal.

I am not like them.

And I sure as hell am not normal.

"I've packed a bag," she continues, briefly looking down at where she's dropped it at her feet.

She's leaving him right now? So why the hell is she over here? I hope she doesn't want to crash here. That would be a huge assumption on her part.

"Okay?" I frown, unclear of my role here. "What about your sons?"

"I need to get on my feet, then I'll come back for them."

Before I can say anything else, she rushes toward me and throws her arms around my neck, catching me off guard and making me teeter on my feet as I'm forced to catch her. It's odd, and I don't know how to respond.

I pat her back, then detach her from me. She looks down at her feet.

"Thank you for always being kind to me," she murmurs. "I wish Eric was more like you."

Once again, I don't understand what she's referring to. I've never treated her with favor, just tried to be polite to keep up appearances. Maybe she's crazy and that's why Eric fucks anything with a pulse. When I don't speak, she appears to take this as an invitation. She advances on me, lifting on her tiptoes and planting her lips to mine.

What the hell is happening?

Her kiss is frantic and starved as her fake breasts smash against me. She's an attractive woman, sure, but she's been worn down by a selfish husband and is famished for affection.

Eric's smirky, cocky face flashes in my mind, and satisfaction settles in my bones. His little wife has left him and she's here with me. I pull her away and look at her smudged lipstick as she pants for air.

So fucking eager.

She's here begging for scraps of affection. Affection she's conjured up in her own mind thinking I'd be willing to give to her. It makes me wonder if she has ever fucked Eric's friends and partners. Levi, maybe not. And Mateo seems happily married. But Trevor? Nixon and his likeness isn't just a coincidence. Julia has been hungry for attention her whole marriage, and Trevor offered it to her at some point. There's no doubt in my mind.

"Please, Jax," she begs.

All I can think about is how smug Eric is about his seemingly perfect life. Yet, look how pathetic his wife is—how eager and needy her cunt is for me. No wonder he finds me so threatening. I bet she moans my name while she touches herself.

Dirty Mrs. Pearson.

She's hungry for me. I'll feed her, then send her back to him, knowing at every party he throws and invites me to, I fucked his deprived wife. It's ammo to store and use against him if the need arises.

I'm not usually a petty man...

Oh, who am I kidding?

Of course I fucking am.

All men are, and I'm no exception.

I swipe the tools from the table I use, causing her eyes to widen with anticipation as they clatter loudly to the floor. She moves to hop on, but I stop her with a hand to her shoulder and a shake of my head. I spin her body around so her back is to me and push her shoulders forward with a heavy palm until she's laying her torso flat against the wood surface. Lifting her little flower emblazoned dress, I stroke over the little scars of stretched skin made only by carrying four children, and fist her expensive underwear, tearing them away with a grunt. She's panting and trembling, so desperate for human contact. To have someone want her, desire her—give her an inkling of attention and prove she's still a woman, not just a mother and wife.

When I kick her legs apart, her cunt opens, and her arousal is pungent. It's been a hot day, and her fuck hole stinks of sweat, so my cock won't harden. I've never been with a woman of her age or who has birthed so many children. I'm learning I don't find her one bit arousing. That's problematic. The idea of Eric jabbing away at her over the years is a turn off and her making those eager noises makes my cock want to disappear inside itself like a second belly button.

I want her to shut up.

Force her to be still.

To do as she's told.

My hand twitches, and I notice I'm still holding the screwdriver in my palm. The handle is made of rubber and shaped like the fat sausages Eric served tonight.

Perfect.

I turn it in my hand so I'm fisting the metal end, then thrust the rubber end of it inside her desperate cunt. There's no barrier. No resistance. It just slides right in, making her scream at the intrusion. Her body becomes rigid compared to the compellability from seconds ago.

She loves it, though. I'm giving her what she needs and she's grateful.

"What is that?" she cries out, looking back at me over her shoulder.

Stop fucking talking, woman.

No wonder Eric's eyes wander. If I had to put my

cock inside her every night, I'd want to run away too.

"Shut up," I bark, holding her down with one hand and using the other to plunder her hole over and over. Juices run down the handle and drip onto my hand. The urge to pull my hand away and swipe it on my slacks is strong, but I grit my teeth and continue my ministrations.

"This is what you want. What you begged for because you don't like the little sluts who parade their under-age asses around for your husband to fantasize about defiling. He likes their tight cunts and smooth skin. Their delicate moans and innocent doe eyes. And there you are, used up, having birthed his sons. You gave the selfish, ungrateful bastard your youth. He wants to eat new pussy while yours dries up."

A sob escapes her as my words hit their intended mark.

"I thought you liked me." She sniffles, grunting.

Why did she think that?

I must be better at this pretending shit than I thought.

"I do," I lie, using my forearm muscles to speed this shit up. I'm already bored and my mind is on other things.

Why did I bother entertaining her in the first place? *To have one over on Eric.* I think this actually may be one he has over me. I'm doing *him* a favor seeing to this chore so he doesn't have to.

"Look how good to you I'm being," I croon in a tone I've heard men use on women. I've learned women are the easiest creatures to manipulate. A few soft words and compliments can usually win over any female.

Her cunt becomes a slippery pit, and gone are the questions. Now she's clinging to the sides of the table, her nails scraping with every prod. She's sobbing, her body jerking from the force of her misery. She wanted to be a whore, and now she's being treated like one.

It's never as you thought it would be, is it?

I snort and pull the object from her, only to realize it's not her arousal making her wet but blood. Maybe I was a little rough. I drop the object to the floor and remove my hand from her back.

"You're welcome," I tell her with a smirk.

Damn, I wasn't just including myself in the neighborly functions, I was now doing charity work on top of it.

Shaking, she gathers herself, pushing down her dress and bending to pick up her destroyed panties. She scrubs a hand over her face to remove the tears of elation. I bet she hasn't been fucked like that before.

She can't look me in the face, knowing what a whore she's been.

Her disgusting fluids are making my fingers sticky, so I move to the sink to finally wash my hands. She doesn't pick her bag up to leave like I hoped, and having her down here in my space is making me fidgety.

Was I supposed to offer her a beverage now or something? Usually this act is played out very differently for me.

She won't stay. She'll run home where she belongs because actually leaving Eric means leaving his money.

It's going to be amusing. Eric will know she's been up to no good when she limps back to him, and it will be something he always questions. Who, where, with what?

A gasp alerts me to her discovering something she shouldn't have. I dry my hands and turn to face her.

Goddammit.

Why did she have to come over here?

Her instincts on who to flee to were way off.

She closes the door to the basement fridge and stumbles backwards. Her foot lands on the screwdriver, tilting her at an askew angle, and she falls to her ass with a thud. Her face is as white as a sheet as shock washes over her.

"You're quite the nosey neighbor," I tisk, shaking my head and stalking toward her.

"I only w-wanted a s-soda," she defends, her voice cracking. She's trembling all over so badly, she looks like a character with a computer glitch. "What is that?" she chokes out, pointing to the fridge.

I crowd over her and shake my head in disappointment.

"Something I wish you hadn't seen."

ONE

J A X

Psychopath red flag
#2
They're Disciplined

Present (Six years later)

SWEAT POURS OVER MY FOREHEAD AND DRIPS FROM my earlobes. My hair is soaking wet and getting in my eyes. I push it back and gasp at the air to ease the burning in my lungs. I've pushed myself this morning to the brink of collapse. I slow my pace and check my heartrate. A hundred and sixty beats per minute. I run every day, sometimes twice, eat clean, and keep my body hydrated. I have the physique of an athlete—my discipline has made sure of that.

The chill in the air gives way to the warming of the sun, the promise of clear skies and blistering heat.

Crouching down, I pretend to tie my shoelace and count in my mind.

One...two...three...

Checking my watch, I sigh with relief when Mary Stubbs leaves on time for work. Her dark hair sashays across her back and the tight skirt she's wearing shows all her curves. She's a cock tease.

She works for a commercial company and is the only female in the building. She knows what she's doing when she squeezes her fat ass into skirts like that. The woman climbed the corporate ladder on sexual harassment claims.

Whore.

Liar.

Cunt.

I watch her struggle to enter her Mini Cooper. She didn't think about her dress choice limitations. Clearly.

When the car pulls out of the drive, I smile and check my sock to make sure I haven't lost my little gift to myself. It's there and brings with it a feeling of empowerment.

Today, I'm God.

A rush of exhilaration floods through me, causing my heart to keep its fast pace. I check the street, already knowing everyone else on this road goes into work later and all are no doubt still sleeping. I've spent time on this street, watching and learning, distracting myself from the one girl I couldn't have right away. *Lucy*

Her name swirls around in my head, teasing my restraint. I thought my new girl would help wash her away from my thoughts, but she refuses to leave, haunting me persistently.

Moving across the asphalt, I slip through the gate that's always left ajar for the two cats they have as pets.

Stupid women. Cats can climb. They don't need coddling

She's in the kitchen when I enter and doesn't even

notice me as I pass her and go to her room.

I'm here, beautiful Stacy.

She's a vision to any eyes witnessing her in her morning haze. Hair in disarray. Skin flushed from sleep. I wish I got more time to spend with her, but being a single parent and business owner makes having relationships hard. I'm here now, though, and we will make these moments count.

Stacy is beautiful, talented, and has this shy act going for her. It is *an act*, though.

I met her at a college day Rowan had dragged me around to. She was the receptionist and although she acted coy, there was this glint in her eye, one that said, *"I want you."* And she does. She became just what I needed, and saved me from taking bad risks with...*Lucy*.

Lucy...Lucy...Lucy, why can't I let you go? And why does he have to be the one who has her? It would have been different with me.

Anyone could fuck her, but that's not what I'm into.

I like the process, the build-up of getting to know all the intricate details that make up her as a person, until we're speaking the same language and I can give her what she wants while taking what I need from her.

Stacy's scent surrounds me, encompassing me, goading me, preparing me. I release Lucy from my mind's grip and give Stacy my full attention like she deserves.

Rowan has been nagging me about getting a woman. She thinks I'll be on my own and lonely when she leaves for college, so when I tell her I have been seeing someone, it will placate her.

I kick off my sneakers and strip my clothes, folding them and placing them on the dresser. The sweat has begun to dry, leaving my skin dewy. The need to get clean is like a voice whispering from the corners of my mind.

I wait for her to return to her room, anticipation building, thickening my cock. Her footfalls are soft over the carpet, but her singing out of tune is not.

Pushing the door open, she places a mug on the

dresser and frowns as she picks up my sneakers.

I step from behind the door and wrap a hand around her mouth, tugging her body against mine and injecting my gift into a small mole on her neck.

Prick.

Done.

Game over.

So simple. So effective. Such a fucking rush.

She doesn't have time to fight. Her mouth opens to scream against my palm, but it's muffled. I slip my other hand around her waist, holding her body firm against my chest.

Her legs weaken from the cocktail of drugs, and she collapses into my torso.

Lifting her, I bring her over to the bed and place her down, straightening out her limbs so she's spread-eagled across the duvet. A vision. Her eyes are wide, and I know there are a thousand things running through her mind, but none of it matters. She's mine now. Her body is mine to manipulate. Control. Own.

It's perfect. She's perfect. We're perfect.

Her hair fans out over her pillow, making her look angelic.

Brushing my hand down her cheek, the softness of her young flesh makes me want her more. I can finally taste her. I've kept us both waiting for so long. Keeping to the shadows as I got to know her. Learning her routines, her ties to this world. When I first saw her, I knew she would be mine. My perfect distraction. She's part of my collection, my girls. Worthy of me.

She's seamless. I need to have her. I've waited long enough.

The good ones are always worth the wait.

"I've come to give you what you want," I tell her, a smile tugging at my lips.

Dragging her bed shorts down her legs, I expose the ripe flesh beneath. I bend down to inhale her cunt. I've imagined what she'd look like this close up. What scent she would have. It's honey. She smells like honeysuckle. She keeps hair on her mound, which is a novelty these days. It tickles my nose and top lip, and I decide right here and now I like it.

She's making little mewling noises, but it's almost completely muted, her tongue refusing to obey her commands to call out.

What would you say if you could speak right now, my lovely?

"I want you."

"Take me."

"Make me yours."

Her body spasms slightly with her efforts to try to move, but it's futile.

Little girl, I need you to be still for me.

I unbutton her nightshirt, pull it down her shoulders, and tug it away from her body. Her tits are impeccable, a full handful, the rosy nipples just the right shade of pink. Her stomach is taut, flaring out at her hips. Slender legs toned from running track in high school are spread before me, and the sight of her bare and laid out all for me makes my cock even harder. Goosebumps pebble over her skin, the tiny hairs raising in awareness.

I spread her legs farther, and she opens up like a budding rose. Tears leak from her eyes, causing a rush of adrenaline to course through me. I climb over her body and swipe them away, kissing her eyelids and licking the path of wet tracks up her cheeks.

She's like a broken faucet. The tears just keep coming. I coat the palm of my hand in her fear and rub it over my throbbing cock.

"Cry for me," I coax. "Cry, cry, cry." I inhale the scent of her apple shampoo from her hair, rubbing my cock firmer. "Mmmm, such a good, good girl."

Her lip twitches and eyes strain so hard, the tiny red blood vessels splinter over the white like a broken vase.

"What?" I ask, stroking her hair. "You need me?" She's so desperate to say *yes*. But she can't. It's good I know what she's thinking.

I place myself at her opening, and without warning, I thrust inside her. She's warm and tight. Her body is soft and supple, the limbs heavy and incompliant. It's perfect. I lay my hand over her heart, feeling as it slows beneath my palm.

Thud...thud....thud.....thud......thud.......thud........

"I gave you medicine that numbs your muscles." I thrust forward, burying my cock to the hilt. "Your heart will slow, then you'll have a heart attack."

I love the sound of skin slapping skin. I lunge harder and harder into her still form. "Can you feel it happening?" I implore, taking all her power with each stab inside her hot, strangling cunt. She's hungry, taking me inside her and squeezing me tight. Her chest rises and falls as she struggles to breathe.

The medical records I hacked show she has a heart murmur. Her death will be a surprise, but not suspicious considering her condition.

Her breathing has become harsh, ragged gasps. She's dying, and it's euphoric to be inside her while she rests on the cusp of life and death.

Let it take you, sweet Stacy.

Her body becomes tense as the drug kicks in to its final stages, she's teetering this way and that. Heat races up my spine. My balls draw tight. I pull from her body just as her chest stops moving and spurt white ribbons of cum over her stomach, decorating her creamy skin. Seeing the wet patches of my seed on her flesh almost makes me come again.

Damn, she's better than I thought she'd be.

The wait was more than worth it. I observe her for a few seconds while the wave of pleasure ebbs from my body. I'm going to miss her.

Climbing from her bed, I open her bedside drawer and take out her purple sex toy she keeps there. I know she pleasures herself with it a few times a week. Especially in the mornings after her rude, noisy roommate wakes her up before leaving for work.

I've watched her through the window as she reaches for it and slips it beneath the covers. The gasp of breath as she pushes it inside herself always made me hard. The writhing in the duvet, the heavy pants and flushed skin caused me to stroke myself for her. She's quite something. The innocent act is her façade. In here, in her room, she's a minx. She's mine. We all wear masks for the outside world.

I leave the toy on the bed in case she's checked for penetration. None of my girls' deaths have ever come into question, I make sure of it.

Pulling away from her, I go to her en-suite to turn on the shower. There are products left out and a towel slung over a wash bin instead of inside it. Why are females so messy?

The steam fills the room almost instantly and the thrashing of the water pelting the glass walls matches the humming high in my head. Nothing else in my life makes me feel the way my girls do. It's addictive, and I'm already thinking about who my next girl will be.

Lucy.

No. I can't.

I come back and carry Stacy into the bathroom. Already thinking of a new girl is unfair to her. She deserves all my devotion. I made her wait long enough for it. Dragging her into the shower, I place her body on the floor. It's small, so she lays at an awkward angle, and I have to stand over her to fit inside with her. I use her soap to clean my cock, then wash my seed from her body. I shower the rest of myself until I'm satisfied I'm clean, then lift her up gently, not wanting to leave any bruised fingerprints. With little effort, I force her body backwards through the shower cubicle glass door. Her weight crashes through the sheer wall, causing it to shatter around her like a Lego tower being knocked over. She lands on the tiled floor with an ungodly thud.

A crimson puddle forms beneath her head, coating

her hair and creating a halo around her. How fitting. She was an angel indeed.

Glass has blemished her beautiful, soft cheeks, causing blood welts there.

She looks so perfect, I debate taking her again, but I know better than to change my plans. To get sloppy is to risk exposure.

I empty the drain of any hair there and take a piss, making sure to flush and wipe the seat. I stand naked while I air dry, then redress in my running gear. I locate the needle and tip from the injection I gave her and stuff it back into my sock. The injection site won't even show a mark. It's why I locate a mole or blemish.

Checking the room to see if there's anything I need to do, I notice the mug of coffee she'd brought in here. She would have had that before her shower. Picking it up, I use the bottom of my shirt to cover my hand, drain the cup, and place it down. I can't help but need to see her one last time before leaving.

The shower has filled the room with steam and continues to rain down, flooding the floor.

I take a knee beside her and lean in to kiss her lips. They're growing cold already, but are still plump and precious.

Goodbye, sweet Stacy.

TWO

J A X

Psychopath red flag
#3
They are liars

ENTER MY HOUSE FROM THE SIDE AND MAKE MY WAY upstairs to wake Rowan. She's already prowling around her bedroom when I get there, and I gulp down the guilt of leaving her alone. I'm still riding my high and feel like I'm vibrating all over. I hate to see her right after leaving one of my girls, but it's something I've learned to deal with over the years. My alter ego slips into place with more ease when it's Rowan because I don't have to pretend to feel around her. I *do* feel. If I could love completely like normal people, it would be for her.

"My little girl is growing up," I say from my doorway,

pride evident in my voice. And I am proud. This unity wasn't one I planned, but look how well I did raising a child. It's amazing what the internet and text books can teach you. They make it almost too easy for people like me. They give us the tools we need to stay under the radar. To fit in among the lesser mortals.

Rowan grins over at me, and the brightness in her smile could rival the sun. She's such a vision. Nothing like her mother, although I've lied to her many times saying so.

She's looking directly at me, and in her eyes, I see love and devotion. My daughter doesn't see the emptiness echoing inside my gut. The darkness lurking in my mind. She will always be Daddy's little girl, only seeing the best in me.

"Hey," she replies, flashing her brilliant white teeth.

I push off the frame of her door and enter her room, holding my arms out to hug her. I can't believe she's eighteen.

She hugs me back with vigor, then starts to pull away. Her eyes drop to a stain I hadn't noticed on my shirt. It's small, but it's there. A blood splatter screaming up at me, and my Rowan has seen it. It must have been when I went back for a last kiss. I knew her skin was broken with the scratches of the glass, but I was careless, foolish. All the high drains from me, anger at myself taking its place.

I've worked my entire life to keep this part of me from her. She will never know the demon who rattles against his cage inside me.

"Did you hurt yourself?" she asks, pointing to the spot with a frown before checking over my body.

My smile and happiness from moments before has extinguished like water on a fire, and she notices the change in me. I can see it in her body tensing slightly. I say the first thing that comes to mind.

"Yeah, shaving."

Her mouth pops open, but then closes. I need to take her mind off it, and off the fact that I want to punch a wall.

"Rowan, how mad at me would you be if I rescheduled your birthday dinner?" I ask, changing the subject. A little part of her light penetrates my heart as she chuckles, and I sigh internally.

"Depends on the reason." She narrows her eyes, playing with me.

Rubbing a hand over the back of my neck, I shrug. "I met this woman recently..."

Her eyes expand and elation flushes her cheeks. "You have a date!" she screeches, a huge smile plastered on her face.

A date? Sort of.

I want to go back and watch from the trees as Mary returns home from work and finds *my* Stacy.

"Something like that." I smirk, giving her the hope she wants so badly of me finding someone. I just wish she could understand I don't need anyone but her.

Her and me is how I like it.

How it will always be.

"Go!" she tells me with a giggle. "And take a shower. You stink."

I return her laugh, lifting the shirt over my head. "I promise I'll make it up to you."

"I know you will."

My gaze flits over to the dollhouse I made her, and a genuine smile lifts my lips. I want to shrink her down and keep her inside that dollhouse, to keep her safe. To keep her from ever learning she lives with Jekyll and Hyde.

I leave her to get dressed and take the stairs two at a time down to the foyer. I grab the fire lighter and march to the back of the house, pushing out the bi-folding doors to the yard. I throw a couple logs onto the firepit and light the thing.

Once the flames ignite, I chuck the shirt into the fire, watching the golden licks pull the fabric into its embrace and turn it to ash.

"You killed someone or something." A voice comes

from behind me. I turn my gaze to his over my shoulder.

The sneaky little bastard. Usually, it's impossible to sneak up on me. Nixon, the only son of Eric's I consider an acceptable friend to Rowan, is standing there brazen and curious.

Curiosity killed the cat, little boy.

His words ring loud in my head. I've never killed a boy before, and his youthful age is too close to Rowan's for me to be comfortable snuffing it out, but if he's seen something he shouldn't, what choice is there?

"I'm kidding, Mr. Wheeler." He smirks and prods a stick into the firepit, helping the fire destroy the remnants of my shirt. Under his breath, he mutters, and in the quiet, I can tell he's counting. Counting what? I don't know.

"What are you doing here?" I growl, grabbing him by the collar of his shirt. Not because I care, but because it's the response I should have and hopefully it will keep him from sneaking around the place.

He's tall, like his father, and there's something glaring

back at me in his eyes. Something so familiar, if I could be unsettled by it, I would be.

It's not fear; it's something worse. It's something I recognize every day in the mirror.

Indifference.

Darkness.

The monster lurking under the skin.

As if the blackness surging through him calms him, the counting grows quiet.

He takes my pause as I study him to his advantage and pushes me off him. He holds up a box and looks up to Rowan's bedroom window.

"I just came to give Rowan her birthday present."

I snatch the box from his hand and point to his house. "Go home. I'll give this to her, and, Nixon?" I shout after him because he's already begun to leave. He looks over his shoulder at me.

"Start using the front door, or I may mistake you for an intruder." I make a gun with my fingers and gesture to the trigger being pulled, making sure to aim it at his head as I mouth, "Bang."

A warning.

"Whatever," he scoffs.

I turn my attention back to the fire, then to the box in my hand, creaking the lid open.

There's a locket inside. A simple white gold heart. I open it, and my body tenses. It's a picture of the woman in the few photos I gave to Rowan of her mother. Except they're not actually of her mother. They're from a clothing catalogue that came in the junk mail. She kept asking about her mother and what she looked like when she was little, so I gave her something to hold onto, to look at and love. The woman had the same coloring as Rowan and she was beautiful, so I laminated the pictures and framed them.

She can never know this deceit. She can never know her mother didn't die during childbirth...well, not in the complication aspect of childbirth.

The picture in the locket isn't one I've given Rowan, so Nixon must know my lies. But to what extent? And how?

I throw the chain into the fire and roll my head over my shoulders, cracking my neck.

He may have to go after all.

THREE

J A X

Psychopath red flag
#4
They don't like social situations

THE LIGHTS FLASH, ILLUMINATING THE STREET AS I creep past in my car. There's an ambulance and one police car. The paramedic is talking to an officer, and the other has a blanket around Mary's shoulders, comforting her.

It will be ruled non-suspicious. I played her defect perfectly against her.

If I pull over and disappear into the tree line, I'll be able to wait and watch the coroner arrive and wheel out her body packed up neatly in a bag.

She's gone.

And *life* goes on.

Without her.

———

When I make it home, Rowan is already turned in for the night. I find some leftover chicken from lunch still in the fridge and whip together a sandwich. The adrenaline eats through your calorie burn like a bitch. Maybe I'm onto a new weight loss method. All the fat housewives just need to kill to get thin.

I smirk to myself at the thought of Mrs. Ringwood from across the street going on a rampage with her cockapoo stuffed in her handbag.

Ha.

I finish my sandwich, then go to the basement and collect all of Stacy's files. The image I keep is of her sleeping. I add it to the other's hidden inside a cookie tin and stash it in the wall space I carved out when I first bought this house. I can't help pulling them out and looking through them. There's one girl not amongst the others, and it torments me. She needs to be with them.

I drop them back in the hiding spot and slot the brick back into place, camouflaging that there's even a space there. I take the rest of the images and documents I accumulated about Stacy to the firepit, checking first that Rowan's bedroom lights are in fact out so I know she's sleeping.

I reminisce with each image I burn until nothing is left but the imprint on my brain and the ashes. A breeze cools my skin, and I sense I'm not alone before anyone makes themselves known.

I don't like being crept up on or watched.

I'm the watcher.

"I know you're there," I announce, rising to my feet and walking over to the bar area I had built out here. I open the beer fridge and grab two bottles, popping the lids off.

Nixon stalks from the corner like a shadow. This is

becoming a habit.

"I left some schoolwork in Rowan's backpack," he lies.

I glower at him. "It's a little late to be skulking around the place in the dark."

"I noticed Rowan wasn't wearing her locket," he says, changing the subject effortlessly.

"You know I didn't give it to her. Let's not play games." I smirk, offering him one of the beers. He takes it and nods toward the firepit.

"More shirts?"

Ha. "Not quite."

"Why does Rowan have pictures of Nina Drake framed in her room believing her to be her mother?" he questions.

I should ask him why he thinks Eric is his dad when he looks just like Trevor Blackstone. Instead, I focus on something more paramount.

"How the fuck do you know what's in Rowan's

bedroom?" I growl.

The tilt of his lips shows his amusement. It's not often I can tolerate company, but Nixon holds his own. He's really good at fitting in around them, even though, deep down, he's not like them—much better at fitting in than I could ever be. But just us guys out here, I feel like I almost don't have to pretend in front of him—like he knows me better than most. The real me, not the me I display for everyone. It's an unusual feeling.

"She tutors me sometimes when I'm struggling in my human relations class." He shrugs like it's no big deal. If it were any of the other boys, I wouldn't believe him, but Nixon is frank. He would say if it was more than that. I admire that about him.

"Next time you need to study, you do it downstairs," I demand.

"You haven't answered the question." He looks over at me from the seat he put himself in. I join him, looking out into the yard. I like the night time. It's where I belong and feel most comfortable.

I grit my teeth. "I don't have to answer your questions."

Does he forget his age and who he's talking to?

"But you do if it was her asking?" He quirks a brow, daring me not to answer so he can run along and tell Rowan I've created a plastic life for her.

"Why haven't you said anything to her yet?" I ask, curious.

He swigs his drink and shrugs his shoulders. "I don't like the thought of hurting her for no reason. That's why I'm asking you."

"How do you even know the woman? What did you call her? Nina Drake?" I query.

He quirks a brow, looking over at me with a sigh of amusement. Digging into his pocket, he pulls out a cell phone, flicks his thumbs over the keys, then hands me the screen.

Well, shit.

Nina Drake, once a small-time model has now turned porn star. This whole time, I've allowed Rowan to have a porn star's image as her mother.

I hand him back the phone. "When Rowan was young, she was desperate to know about her mother. But she and I were never a couple. Rowan was an accident. One I didn't know about until her mother was dying and she was born. I didn't want her knowing that, so I gave her a mother to hold onto. You can relate, right?" I ask.

His features don't change, not even a flinch of pain. "Rowan's mother died, mine fucked off."

"Do you ever wonder why?"

He snorts. "Because my old man likes younger pussy. He can't let it go, though. He's still searching for her. I don't give a shit if he finds her. She made her choice."

Eric is still looking for Julia? Well, that is news.

Nixon stands and tosses his empty bottle in the trash. "Lucky for you, Rowan's not a boy, so she won't watch much porn." He winks and saunters off.

I watch as he disappears though the entrance they made years ago. I closed it up at one point, but the little fucks reopened it. Jumping to my feet, I go grab a hammer and nails to seal the thing shut. Again.

FOUR

J A X

Psychopath red flag
#5
They are overly charming

FIND MYSELF BACK IN THE BASEMENT, PULLING OUT the files I kept of Lucy. Memories of when I first found her brighten my mind like search lights seeking her out in the dark sea of my mind.

Nine months ago

Throwing some onions into the pan, I brown them and add the cooked chicken. I like to cook for Rowan. A balanced diet is important, and it gives my mind reprieve from thinking about finding my next girl. I haven't found anyone since

Rebecca, and it's making me jittery.

"Hey, Daddy," Rowan says, coming into the kitchen and sitting on a stool opposite where I'm preparing dinner. "What would you say to me and the Pearson boys staying at one of Mr. Blackstone's beachfront properties for the summer?"

My hand slows the stirring and my head begins to haze with a storm rumbling within it. She's so casual with her words, reaching forward and swiping a fresh piece of pepper from the chopping board and popping it in her mouth like she's just asked me for a pony.

"Is that a joke?" I ask. Because clearly, she's fucking joking.

"He owns like the entire seafront. Well, all but one Hayden said, but he has a different one he said we could use over the summer months. It's totally safe. The boys and I thought—"

"No!" I snap, the spatula slapping against the counter. She startles and looks to where my hand grips the handle. My knuckles are white. "You're seventeen. A child."

The boys and I thought. Goddamn those little bastards.

"Daddy?" she breathes. "Please? You know them. Nothing

is going to happen."

"You and four boys, Rowan? Do you know what people would say? What those boys will try?"

Her eyes narrow on me, and her lips draw into a thin line. "That's not fair. They're my friends."

"The answer is no," I warn. "Now, wash up for dinner."

She huffs and slips from the stool. "I already ate pizza over at Eric's house."

"Eric?" I fume. "It's Mr. Pearson to you, and I don't like the amount of time you've been spending over there lately."

Her cheeks burn pink, and her hand rests on her hip as she glares at me. Not like my precious Rowan, but like a moody teenager. She thinks she's grown just because she'll be a senior this year. Her mother looked at me like that once too. Once.

"I'm nearly an adult." She stomps her foot, as if reading my mind. God forbid if she ever were able to actually read my mind. What a chaotic minefield that would be.

"I know how old you are, but no matter your age, I'll always be your father and looking out for your best interests,"

I try to placate, but I've learned over the years reasoning with a child is nearly impossible. Especially a teenage girl.

"You mean controling me?" she bites out.

Who is the girl standing before me?

It's like she's becoming someone else overnight.

Definitely been spending too much time with the little assholes next door.

"If it comes to that, then yes," I warn.

Her eyes widen in defiance.

"Eric...I mean, Mr Pearson said he could stay there too to keep an eye on us," she pushes the issue.

"Rowan," I warn. "The answer is no."

I've never wanted to be tough on her, but if she forces my hand, I'll take steps to keep her in line. She's not ending up like Eric Pearson's kids—or under them, for that matter. Their influence is spreading through my sweet Rowan like a disease and I'll cut those fuckers out like one too.

Her eyes water, and I hate to see that look on her face. She's the only person who can bring me to my knees. She will thank me one day for being firm with her when it comes to those boys, though.

"I'm going to bed," she announces, swiping her face as tears leak out before storming out of the room and up the stairs.

Something has to change. Maybe Eric needs a warning, not Rowan. If he pushes me, he better be prepared for the shove he gets in return. How dare he make her think it's okay to abandon me and stay with him and his four sons—to get the whole town talking and casting their eyes our way. No. Fuck no. It's not happening.

———

I finish the chicken stir-fry on my plate and clean the kitchen before booting up my laptop and checking out Trevor Blackstone's properties. The fact that there's one he doesn't own intrigues me, and could be a potential opportunity for me to purchase and rub it in his face if the need ever arise.

I note down the address and add it to my list of things to do tomorrow.

———

Trevor Blackstone, property tycoon at the rate he's going with all these investments. These beachfront properties are a gold mine, and he owns all but one—the one I've been staring at for the past twenty minutes. I skipped my morning run to stake out this place and although my legs are already getting jittery, it's been worth it. You can learn a lot by just watching. Waiting. Biding your time.

The woman who used to own this house was ancient. When I looked her up, she was nearly ninety by the time she died. From my research, I discovered the property is in the name of a trust. Trevor is beyond rich and could afford to offer her any price, so why is the trustee not selling? I couldn't find any other useful information, which is why I'm here to get a closer look.

I ponder staking out the place, seeing if the trustee took possession of the home. I might slip inside and hold a pillow over the unsuspecting fuck's face in the middle of the night.

That way, I could see what happens with the property and take the next step to acquiring it before Trevor can.

I may have a better chance with the trustee still breathing, however. I could just convince them to sell to me.

I'm about to get out my car to go sweet talk the new owner, which I'm hoping is a woman. No female has resisted my charms in the past eighteen years, and one way or another, I always get what I want. This place could be for Rowan. She wanted the beach, and I could give it to her. A gift for me upsetting her at dinner last night. One rule. No boys. Not a harsh rule for such a prize. She could stay here on weekends, and that would give me more privacy and stop the pack of animals next door from trying to sneak over.

I open the car door, but falter when I see a petite auburn-haired female walking toward the house.

My stomach coils in a good way, and a sigh passes my lips. Pulling the door closed, I just watch her through the pane of glass, transfixed by her. My soft intake and exhale of breath is the only sound around me.

God, who is that?

Is she the one who now owns the old woman's house?

She's wearing tiny jean shorts and a tank top that shows a sliver of her taut, tanned stomach. Her hair is pulled up on top of her head, but some strands have fallen free, framing the delicate features of her face.

She saunters rather than walks, a sway to her hips, a carefree, confident swagger to her movements. The world stops and she's all there is. My heart races, and my palms sweat.

If she's the one I need to encourage to sell, this whole idea just got ten times more intriguing.

She's holding a cell phone to her ear and shaking her head, not happy with whoever is on the other end. With a huff, she ends the call, but still shouts at her phone animatedly before disappearing inside the old woman's house. Out of my sight, she slips away, and I feel like I've fallen through a rabbit hole. I'm tumbling, my head dizzy.

My heart rate has increased, and my cock hardens. It's a feeling I've become accustom to when the need overtakes me.

The urge, the overwhelming ache that grips me, strengthening until the only thing I know is...

I need her. Want her. Must have her.

A relieved breath leaves my body. I've found my new girl, finally.

And she's perfect. No, she's magnificent.

The good ones are worth the wait. This one, I could wait years for. Just watching and learning her every move. It would be so fucking sweet when I finally made my move.

She will be mine.

All mine.

I wait all day and night for my chance to inspect. Patience is a virtue.

Darkness has crept over the sky, shadowing the road I'm parked on. The streets are empty, and the lull of the ocean is the only sound outside the window of the car. Opening the door, I step outside and pop the trunk, taking out my camera from my stashed emergency bag.

I move to the brush by the side of the houses and then down onto the beach they overlook. Sand fills my shoes, and I curse myself for not going home to change before doing this. But I couldn't risk her leaving and me not seeing where she goes. Maybe she's just visiting and won't be back for weeks, months, years? I can't afford to let her fall through my grasp without knowing anything about her.

She's mine.

My heart hammers in my chest when I see her through the window. She's clearing things away and dancing to music muted to my ears. She's young, carefree, beautiful. Mine. Mine. Mine.

Click. Click. Click.

I watch her through the lens that zooms right into the room as if I'm within reaching distance. Like I can just reach out and touch that soft, silky, golden skin. Feel her beneath my fingertips. Smell her. Breathe her in. Run my hands through the strands on her head. I'd strip her from that shirt and enjoy the bounce of those ripe, firm tits, then I'd remove those tiny barely-there shorts. I bet she's clean-shaven. Soft, rosy flesh hidden away in plump, juicy folds. I'll open her up, unwrap her like a prize. She'll want it, beg with her eyes, "Take me." And I will. I'll take her. All of her. Until her last breath.

Eventually.

But for now, I watch and learn.

I wait.

So worth it, this one.

The lights suddenly turn off, plunging the house in darkness, my view robbed from me.

Fuck.

Checking my watch, I see it's past eleven in the evening. Rowan springs into my mind.

Dammit.

I should have been home hours ago, but I became too consumed.

Giggling sounds from a little way up the beach, and a deep, throaty voice shushes whoever is lurking out here. That's my cue to leave. I mustn't be seen here at night with a camera. It's sloppy. I've been too careless spending the day parked in one spot, and it's got to stop. I can't get careless now.

Once I hit the asphalt again, I empty my shoes and sling them in a bag before tossing it in the trunk. I drive home barefoot, determined to return when the time is right.

To watch, wait, take.

Present...

I breathe hard and stuff the images away. I kept all the data I collected because I assumed I would have taken her by now. But she became too high risk. Part of me knew I would always return for her; she's too special not to have and reminds me so much of my first girl, the one I picked out just for me, the one who started my collection.

She was Rowan's babysitter's best friend. It's amazing the things people tell you when they're distraught. Her best friend was ill, suffering. The pretty little thing known as Aimee had severe asthma and had been having more attacks than usual. It was perfect really. It gave me the idea of hiding my urges and the consequences of those urges, a body count, in plain sight. If I could make her death look like the result of natural causes, it could be the perfect crime.

And so my collection began. At night, I would feed my darkness, and during the day, I would feed my daughter. Both worlds, both versions of me existing together.

But Lucy wasn't Aimee. She didn't have an illness, and she had become too intricate in the lives of those around me. It was seeing Lucy with Rowan one day at the middle school when Brock's car broke down after picking up the youngest one that stopped me pursuing her.

Rowan was there talking animatedly to my sweet Lucy, and I became solidified to my seat. I couldn't even get out the car. I drove away and sent a tow for them instead.

It was bad enough that I'd learned about her and Trevor, but her being part of Rowan's world? It was all

FIVE ───────────

J A X

too close—too risky. It became clear, no matter how much she was fated to be mine, I couldn't have her.

Psychopath red flag
#6
They have a grandiose sense of self worth

URGES ARE SO POWERFUL. THEY CAN RULE THE mind, the body, and the soul. Mine is a living and breathing entity, burrowed inside me, and if I don't allow it to come out and feed, I'll not only lose myself, but my grip on sanity. The pull of this woman, my lovely Lucy, is stronger than any before her. I knew she was special, but also knew I couldn't have her...then, now...

Yes, you can.

If I could, when I can, I'll have to take my time with her, savor the chase, the build-up, the agonizing wait.

I will wait as long as it takes.

But my beast will need to feed on her eventually, and she will love every second of it. The urges are coming more frequently these days. I've been thinking about her, re-looking over the data of her, the pictures. Fuck. I worry whether I'll be able to juggle all aspects of my life if the tempo increases further. Sacrifices will have to be made to sustain the hunger, and I'm not sure I'm ready to sacrifice anything I've built over the years.

I shouldn't be here, but I need to feel her around me. I'm back in the shop where I first introduced myself to her.

Past...

The sun is burning down, making me squint. I walk across the sand, wincing from the heat of the granules baking under the rays all day. She's coming toward me, but looking down at the water. I will her to see me, look at me, and my breath hitches when her eyelids flutter and her head turns toward me just as I pass her. Fuck, so close, yet so far. I walk a few more yards, then backtrack. I stay at a distance and bide my time.

I follow her into a small shack-like shop, my heart galloping at the possibility of what will happen when she sees me for the first time. I'm so close now, if I reach out, I'll be touching her. This close, I can see her so clearly. I know it was fate that she was given to me. She will be my favorite, and hard to top once I take her and feel her die under me. God, I want to keep her, but the last one I kept was discovered, and it didn't end well. Not for Julia, anyway.

She's studying the refrigerators, her nose crinkling from the overpowering scent of fish. It's so cute, I want to whip out my phone and capture the moment to fuck my hand to later.

"You get used to it after a while," I tell her, moving closer so I can inhale her perfume. It's sweet like her. She smells of summer and frosting.

I don't normally engage with my girls before I take what's mine, but with her, I can't help it. She's different. Special. Mine.

She looks up at me, a brief spark of recognition from passing me on the beach once before. "Oh yeah, sorry. Not used to the fish smell. Where I come from, it's normally already dead and wrapped in a pretty seal and probably pumped with tons of chemicals..." she rambles. "Okay! So, hi. I think I just saw you on the beach. Are you a local?" she continues, anxiously.

Fuck, she's a talker. Making her silent will bring me more pleasure knowing this simple fact. She checks me out, not subtly at all, and I know she likes what she sees. I wore shorts and a fitted T-shirt, showing off my impressive physique just for her. Her stomach will be humming with need and juices dribbling from her cunt, begging to be tasted. I'm easy on the eyes, and my structure always has women thinking about my stamina in the bedroom. They want to be picked up and thrown against a hard wall every now and then, and my strength can send their *mind spinning with possibilities.*

Shit, she asked me a question. What was it? Oh, yes, am I local?

"You can say that. I live not too far away. And you?" I ask, already knowing full well where she lives or resides for the time being.

"Oh, I'm not from here. Well, I am now. Or for the next month." She becomes flustered, tripping over her words. Her cheeks burn bright. "I'm staying here for the summer." She chews on her bottom lip, and my cock stirs. When I have her one day, I'll chew on that lip as well.

Just the summer. At least I know the time scale I have to work with. This is disappointing, but not a game changer. I can't not have her now, even if I only have a week to execute my plans.

I curve my lips into a smile and take another step toward her until we're impossibly close. I can sense the rise and fall of her chest, the heart behind her ribs pounding as I reach in front of her and grab a box from the shelf.

"Well, welcome to the neighborhood..." I linger on the last word, waiting for her to fill in the blank.

"Lucy. The name's Lucy."

Oh, sweet Lucy. My lovely. It's so fitting—so innocent and light. So perfect for her, for me. Mine. My lovely Lucy.

She offers her hand, and I grasp it and bring it to my lips, placing a kiss there and stroking her pulse point. I refrain from inhaling, from sighing and tugging her closer. In time, I'll do all those things. I already know how badly she craves me. She wants me to drag her into me, lift her onto the freezer, and tilt her ass on the edge. She'll be quivering and soaking wet, begging, "Please." Her hands want to roam and touch places I won't allow. I need her still, under the mercy of my touch. I need to feel her pulse weaken, her chest slow its movements. I have to be inside her on the cusp of life and death—give her a moment others will never get.

Oh, lovely Lucy, you will have me, and it will be perfect.

"Pleasure meeting you, Lucy." And it's the most honest I've ever been with anyone in my entire life.

She's different. She is perfect.

"All right, my darling!" The old, decrepit woman who runs the shop steps between us. "You'll make a great meal with these two. Make sure to come back again soon for more seafood."

Lucy smiles down at the woman before bringing her eyes back to mine, a spark ignited there. I almost want to stuff the old woman in the freezer and watch her body crystalize for interrupting our moment, but I'm already lost in lovely Lucy once more.

"Lobster night." She grins, holding up the box the old woman gave her.

"I see." I raise a brow. The compulsion to lean in and bite her bottom lip until it breaks under my teeth makes my head swim. I'm heady, and my cock is straining so hard against the zipper of my shorts, it will have a mark when I take the fucking things off later.

She hovers for a moment, unsure what to do next, then pats the box and gives me a half wave. "Well, it was nice meeting you, uh..."

"Jax," I tell her, then scold myself internally. I shouldn't have given her my real name. This one is different from my usual girls, though. I've never seeked out an interaction before. Usually, I meet my girls at random and keep a distance. It's safer that way.

"Got it. Jax. Well, hope to see you around!"

You will, lovely little Lucy. I will be the last thing you ever see.

"Oh, I hope so too," I agree, my words almost slurred. I'm so high on her allure, it's like being drunk.

I close my eyes, breathing in the last scent of her sweet perfume, ignoring the raw fish pungent in the air around me before I leave her.

Don't worry Lucy, I'll be back soon.

Present...

I go back to my car and slip into the driver's seat and free my cock, stroking it hard in my firm grip. The actions are torturous and punishing as I picture Lucy bound by invisible ropes. A prisoner inside her own paralyzed body, naked, spread wide, and desperate for me to finally claim her. I'm just about to come, but I stop my movements before I do. The throbbing ebbs, and the eager need to come is so built up inside, my body slowly withdraws. It takes ten full seconds for me to breathe through the ache before I stuff my cock back inside my shorts. When I finally do come, it will be with her in sight, not in thought.

I need to have her. I will just have to make sure I plan it out perfectly.

SIX

J A X

Psychopath red flag
#7
They are cunning

WAITING IS DIFFICULT FOR MOST. IT'S A TEST to one's character. A measure of a man's strength. For me, waiting isn't so much a nuisance or a punishment. It's a reward—makes something sweet even sweeter.

And for her, I wait.

Sometimes, the challenge in waiting is half the excitement. The building that slowly grows inside you becomes like a living, breathing beast. When the time is right, I will unhook that beast's chain and let him run fee.

The waiting will be over. Finally.

She's waiting. She'll be ready.

The bacon sizzles, lifting the aroma into the air and enticing Rowan from her room. Her soft footfalls sound on the stairs before her petite frame rounds the door.

There's a crimson blush to her cheeks and a dazed look in her eyes. She must have slept well.

"Hey, Daddy."

She winces when she takes a seat. Maybe she's coming down with something.

She was asleep when I got home last night, her door shut and lights out. It gave me time to go over some new information I'd gathered and the old photos. To study them in critical detail, but there was not one imperfection I could see. There never is. Even after all this time, after thousands of pictures I've taken of her, I can't seem to find one thing wrong with her. Aside from her living arrangements and the company she keeps, she's perfect. Thoughts of my sweet, waiting girl kept me awake until the early hours of the morning. I stroked my cock until it screamed for release, then punished myself with a cold shower. Becoming undone by my new girl isn't allowed. I must keep my wits about me, discipline my urges.

But the longer I wait, the harder it is to keep control. The desire to storm into her life like a hurricane is becoming impossible to ignore.

I place breakfast in front of Rowan and go to the medical cabinet to fetch the thermometer.

"Open," I order, holding the stick at her mouth.

Dark lashes fan out above her eyelids as her eyes expand. "What are you doing?" she admonishes, pushing away my hand.

"You look different. I thought you were feeling unwell."

The crimson flush grows brighter as her eyes drop to her breakfast. She picks up a piece of toast and darts from the stool and out of the room.

There's a small smearing of blood on the seat she's vacated. She must have her period. I'll make sure to pick her up some Tylenol and candy while I'm out today. I check the calendar where I have her cycle marked and discover her period is early. I always monitor her cycle so I can buy her the correct products and get in the ice cream she likes around that time of the month. I learned this from a TV show when she was just reaching puberty, and it fared me well over the awkward hormonal times. Maybe this sort of thing happens as they get older. I'll have to read up on it later.

I gather her heating pad and take it to her room. She's talking in hushed whispers as I push open her bedroom door. She startles and drops her cell phone when she notices she's no longer alone.

"Daddy!" she screeches, her brows pulling down over her eyes. She's been acting strange this week. Like she's hiding something. I know she thinks her relationship with one of the Pearson boys is a secret, but I know everything about her. So long as he's not fucking my daughter, she can have her teenage crush.

I raise the heating pad to show her I'm just bringing her something, and she frowns deeper.

"I thought you may need this," I clarify.

"Why?" she scoffs.

We stare at each other for a few seconds in silence. I must have been wrong. Maybe it wasn't blood. *It was blood.*

"It doesn't matter. Get ready. I'll take you to school."

"I'm leaving early today," she tells me. "I'm going to the middle school for a reading program."

The middle school.

Where my lovely spends her days teaching music and making children smile.

It's fate. It's fucking fate.

A thrill of excitement courses through me.

"That's fine. I will take you, sweetheart. I'll be downstairs when you're ready." I leave her to get ready and stuff the heating pad away in a cupboard.

Pouring the remains of my coffee down the sink, I

rinse my mug and scowl when I see a woman sneaking out of the Pearson's residence. It's not unusual to see women fleeing that place, but this girl seems younger than the rest.

Damn, I'm lucky my Rowan is a good girl.

I don't have enough digits to count on both hands the harem of women pouring out of Eric's bed over the years. He doesn't even try to hide it. He's proud of sucking the singles market bare. Using up the desperate girls with stars in their eyes and discarding them like trash once his cock's dry and limp.

I don't understand the appeal he has. It's grotesque, his pursuit of women half his age, and his boys are following in his footsteps with regards to fucking anything that flashes their ass their way. I'll be damned if I let Rowan become one of their dirty conquests.

"Ready?" Rowan asks, coming up behind me. "What are you looking at?"

"Just one of Eric's playthings," I growl.

Her breath hitches, and she moves me out of the way to look out the window.

"She's gone," I state, annoyed Rowan is witnessing one of his whores leaving. I don't want her thinking that's acceptable behavior.

The walk of shame isn't one she'll ever be taking.

I wait for her to get her fill of the antics of the neighbor, but she's transfixed.

Why are teenagers so nosey?

"Come on, Rowan," I bark. "You know how I hate tardiness."

Swiping up my keys and briefcase, I open the front door, but Rowan hasn't followed me.

"Rowan?" I call, and get no response. Going back to the kitchen, I find her still staring outside, but it's now at Eric berating Hayden. Maybe the girl wasn't one of Eric's whores, after all. Eric's still wearing pajamas. He must be skipping the office today, no doubt making Trevor pick up the slack. Rowan turns to me, her arms wrapping around her stomach.

"What's wrong?" I ask, dropping the case and going to her. I take her in my arms and hold her. Her hands grip onto my shirt, and in this moment, she's back to being my little girl.

"I think you were right, Daddy. I don't feel well. Can I just stay home today?"

I release her and place a hand to her head. She's not warm, but she wouldn't fake feeling unwell. "Okay. Go to bed. I'll bring you some chicken noodle soup at lunchtime from Margo's."

She smiles before reaching up on her tiptoes and kissing my cheek. "Thank you." And then, she's running into the foyer. She comes back with a bag and hands it to me as if she's eager to see me off. "Would you be able to drop this off at the middle school office? It's for that reading thing."

Auburn hair. Sweet curves. Adorable smile.

Mine. Mine. Mine.

"Sure." I take the bag filled with books and kiss her forehead. I can only hold back my grin of anticipation for so long and barely make it out of the room before it breaches my face.

———

My mind can't focus on my lovely, no matter how much I've missed her, when I know my Rowan is home feeling ill. Maybe she's coming down with the stomach flu. A churning in my gut reminds me of the time she was eight or nine and vomited for two days straight. I don't lose my cool often, but cleaning up a kid's puke for days is enough to drive any single parent to madness.

Pulling into the middle school, I pass Trevor Blackstone's over-the-top sports car.

His son is grown and in college. There's only one reason he would be here—to see what's mine. I clutch the steering wheel to keep from ramming his car with mine, killing him on impact.

He frowns as he passes me, doing a double take. I'm getting a little fed up with the attitude Eric and his partners aim toward me, especially Trevor. He has everything, and he doesn't even realize it. Well, for now, anyway. Soon, he will have nothing. It must be hard having another man in their circle, especially one superior to them, but it's not like I ask to be invited to their shindigs. I prefer them to be a square and for me to be singular. Eric forces this weird acquaintance on me where he pretends to be friendly but waves his metaphorical dick around the entire time. It's not friendship, that's for fucking sure. I can't stand him, and I know it's mutual. He just doesn't have a real reason to dislike me, not one he would ever admit to anyway. The only conclusion I've ever come up with is he's jealous I'm better looking, successful, and a hell of a lot of a better father than he could ever dream of. Quite simply, he feels threatened by my superiority.

I manage not to smash Trevor as he leaves the school and find that worthy of a motherfucking pat on the back for as much restraint as it took. The memories of when I discovered he had tricked my woman into being with him assault me, making me hit the brakes.

Past...

I'm back on the beach. I'd overheard her talking on her cell phone yesterday about going for a walk on the beach and planned my entire day around being here so we could "bump" into each other again. But I never for the life of me expected to see her with company, and not just any company. Trevor Blackstone of all people. There's something between them. It's evident in their postures and closeness. Fucker wormed his way in, no doubt for the same reason I stalked the house in the first place—to learn who owned it and how to acquire it.

Even though he's with her, I can't help but still want to be close to her, to watch her lips move as she speaks and smell her flowery scent. I will take great pleasure in watching him squirm knowing the old fuck has some competition. Her cunt will get wet from the mere sight of me, something Trevor no doubt has no abilities of doing.

I'm waiting for you, my lovely. Don't worry.

She's staring directly at me, and she must have said something to Trevor because he's squinting, trying to see what or whom she's talking about.

It's me, motherfucker. Boo!

As they get closer, Trevor's frown makes him look old. She's way out of his league, and he knows it. He senses the threat I am. How could he not? He's been punching above his weight, and she'll outgrow him with or without me in the picture.

"I knew I recognized you," Lucy says, her smile as dazzling as the sun. "Jax, right?" She already knows it's right. And now he knows I'm in her life. This could be a problem.

My cock stirs knowing she hasn't stopped thinking about me. Dreaming of me. I've watched her in her room at night touching her body, looking at herself in the mirror, pretending she's performing for me. Sometimes, when she looks out the window, I think she knows I'm out there looking back and her body trembles and quakes, begging for me to make that night the night—the night I finally take her as mine.

What has me truly excited is my company has acquired a new untraceable drug I will be trying out on Lucy when the time is right. It was all lining up like fate until this wrench in the cog.

"That's right. Good memory, Lucy." I give her a lopsided grin, a knowing one that will make Trevor question how she knows me. I stand closer than I should so he can smell my cologne, and so she can taste it on her tongue. His small mind will be racing and conjuring up dirty images of me fucking her—images the crazy bastard won't be able to escape from. He'll no doubt accuse her of them rather than ask her, and they will argue. Perfect. I could go to town on her without using any drugs, getting things messy and bloody, then pining it on Trevor.

God, my cock is so hard at the mere idea.

"Trevor," I greet, keeping the venom from my tone.

"Jax," he replies curtly.

Lucy's eyes bulge, and she turns her head abruptly to Trevor.

"Wait, you two know each other?" she gasps, and it's a beautiful sound. One I want to hear in my ear as I enter her body.

Dear little Lucy, he is the reason you will be mine. If it weren't for him, I would have never have driven down to check out the property in the first place. Fate.

"Jax is Eric's neighbor," he states, staring at me like he can dissect me. Many have tried. Many have failed. I should be offended of how he says I'm just Eric's neighbor, like that's all I am, like we haven't been forced into social situations many times before this and he's known me for six years.

Trevor's jaw tenses, then he reaches out, clasping Lucy's hand in ownership. A pathetic show of a weak man.

The sizzle of heat and urge to punch him in the throat, crushing his windpipe, slithers through me, but I swallow it down. Bide my time.

"What brings you out here? Bit out of the way for you,"

Trevor accuses, tugging Lucy to him.

Pitiful.

How she isn't laughing at his lame-ass attempt of who has the bigger cock is beyond me. And it's me, by the way. I have the biggest cock, and it will be buried inside her soon enough.

I smile at him, which makes his eye twitch. A droplet of sweat slides down the side of his aging face, then my eyes graze over Lucy and all that tanned skin on display for my viewing.

"Just enjoying the views," I tell him, my eyes never leaving Lucy's form. It's so easy to rile him up. He's so insecure, it's almost embarrassing.

"Okay, well. Great running into you again. Trev promised to fill me up on yummy food, amongst other things, so...we better get goin'," Lucy rushes out, clearly uncomfortable being on the arm of this idiot.

I keep my smile firmly in place despite the numerous ways I'm planning on disemboweling Trevor.

He marches her off without a goodbye, but she turns with pleading eyes. "Make me yours."

I will, my lovely. Don't you worry. Soon.

Present...

I left the beach that day feeling even more determined to make Lucy mine. Trevor is such a weasel, it's criminal he gets to be with her, holding her. On the other hand, that's not what I want from her. I don't want walks on the beach and handholding. I want to own her, mind, body, and soul—own her so completely, I take her last breath. She will be a part of me forever. He could never have that, but all those plans went out the window after seeing her and Rowan together. Then I found Stacy, and it seemed right to wait, but it looks like Trevor isn't going anywhere, and I know I won't be able to just wait around. The voice inside is whispering too strong.

And Rowan hasn't ever mentioned her since. It was just a coincidence. Them being in the same place at the same time, a conversation struck up out of politeness.

Finding a parking spot is easy compared to Rowan's school since none of these kids are old enough to drive. I heave the bag out of the trunk and wonder how my little girl was supposed to lug this thing around with her. It nearly weighs as much as she does.

The security is lacking considering the price these schools charge to send your children here. I manage to get inside without being stopped or questioned. The corridors are long and filled with children.

Damn, this is a nightmare.

The noise of their chatter bounces from the walls. Lockers slam closed, shattering the air around me, making me cringe. It's all too loud here. I hate being surrounded by people, and it's worse when they're teenagers. Even worse than that, middle schoolers.

Horrors of my youth torment me.

A bell shrills, and a flurry of running feet sound in all directions as they hurry to close. And then, I see her through the sea of heads. My lovely girl in waiting. Like a vision plucked from my imagination.

It would be so easy to walk over to her, toss her over my shoulder, and force her into my car. Within hours, she would be gasping her last breath as I fucked her sweet cunt that would weep only for me. She no doubt dreams of a real man —not some old, crazy rich fuck—to stretch her pretty, slippery holes to the point of pain. I would show her everything before I took everything.

Unfortunately, now's not the time. This has to be right.

Tick. Tick. Tick.

I'll wait as long as I must.

She's worth it.

My heart thuds, and the need to go to her, smell her, hear her voice, feel her skin overwhelms me to the point I almost spoil everything.

She's my fate—I know it to be.

I push past the thinning crowd, marching toward her, but then someone grabs my arm, and I find myself turning to face an older man.

"Can I help you?" he asks, his brows furrowed, his drooping skin over his eyelids crinkling as he sweeps his eyeballs over me.

"No," I tell him, then turn around again, finding her straight away and locking my gaze down. She's wearing a sexy little skirt that shows off too much skin. Her tanned legs are toned and smooth, and I want to see them spread before me.

She turns, her auburn strands shielding her face from me.

"Sir?" I'm tugged by the arm again and find it extremely rude. I have to hold back from snapping this old fool's neck.

I turn reluctantly and eyeball the annoying flea distracting me. "I'm dropping off books," I growl.

He swallows and takes a step back, sensing the grim reaper inside me lying dormant, waiting. The corridors have emptied, and I shoot my gaze back around, but she's gone.

Goddammit.

"Where did that lady go?" I demand. I've never been inside her workplace before and I'm desperate to know which classroom is hers. I'm dying to see her full tits jiggle as she gestures to the board, teaching all the rich nitwits at this school about music—something they won't give too shits about when they're running empires like most of their parents in this overpriced school.

The old man looks in the direction I gesture to and frowns. "What lady?"

Fucking idiot.

"The lady who *was* just there." I narrow my eyes.

"I don't know, sir, but you can't be walking the corridor without permission. You need to go through the office and get a visitor's badge."

"No, I don't. Here," I tell him, handing him the bag.

He harrumphs when they hit him in the chest and he almost drops them, not expecting the weight to be so heavy. I march down the corridor and out into the parking lot. Tonight. Tonight I will go to her.

———

It's his house she returns to after work, but he's late coming home and she takes an hour swimming in the sea after the sun has set. Has he never told her about the dangers of being alone on the beach at night, especially swimming in the water? Thunder rumbles across the sky, igniting a fire inside my chest.

What if she disappeared while swimming? Lost to the current, her body dragged out into the open ocean... she could wash up anywhere—or nowhere because she will be with me. But with the evidence suggesting she went for a late-night swim left on the beach, the house open, and a wine bottle drained...Trevor would be left to believe she went drunk swimming. And even if there were an investigation, without a body, there isn't a crime, and they would look at him before ever casting their eyes my way. It's perfect. No illness required.

I watch her run back up the beach, grabbing her towel and bolting into his house.

Creeping up to the house, I spy her inside checking her cell phone, then she turns to something behind her. Trevor. He's home. That's my cue to leave.

SEVEN

J A X

Psychopath red flag
#8
They are emotionally shallow

ROWAN AND I ARE LIKE PASSING SHIPS AS OF LATE. The last weeks of school have kept her busy, and when she's not at school, she's spending time with the Pearson boys. My threats and plans to keep them apart are failing. If I weren't so caught up in my old obsession, lovely Lucy, I would put Rowan on lock down.

My daughter is eighteen now and will soon be off to college. I won't be able to protect her from the predators of this world and that thought alone leaves a pain in my gut like I've swallowed a stone and it's just sitting inside me.

But it's fact.

She will fly the nest and leave me to my own devices.

My sneaking around and watching Lucy will be something I can give my entire focus to. Everything is evolving and changing. Rowan is turning into a woman with hopes, dreams, and a future at her fingertips. And I have my urges that grow more intense by the day.

I pick up dinner from a takeout health deli Rowan likes, but come home to an empty house. I place her food in the fridge and go over to my computer to input the data I've collected, updating Lucy's routines, her swimming preferences and frequency.

With the house she now lives at being on the beachfront, it's heaving with people nearby during the day and evening times, so I've had to spend a lot of time calculating the average visitors to the beach at night, which are almost none. Occasionally, kids will sneak down there, but farther down away from the houses, they're usually too busy drinking and fucking each other to even notice my presence.

The most difficult thing about my sweet Lucy that nearly sends me into a rage of exploring Trevor Blackstone's blood and brain matter is they're a couple. Well, he's trying his best, but she's not fulfilled. That much is evident. If she were, she'd be wearing his ring, last name, or carrying his fucking kid. But she's not. She's waiting for me while passing her time with him. That sandal wearing idiot is a fling. Lucy is probably just being kind knowing he'll kick the bucket at any time since he's an old motherfucker. Just like his friends, he thinks his dick has magic powers and will keep a perfect woman like Lucy forever tethered to him. He's been around Eric fucking Pearson far too long.

Why did she have to be with one of those Four Fathers' fuckers? I've planned out a hundred different ways to kill Trevor, but it's all too risky. When a man of his wealth dies, it automatically raises suspicion. Instead, I will work around him and use his neglect of her to my advantage. The more she's alone, the more time I have to fulfill her.

Lucy is mine and the plan is still in play.

The front door opens and closes, and I watch from the corner of the room as Rowan sneaks inside and up the stairs. The urge to hammer her windows shut and bolt a lock on her bedroom door is strong. I know she's seeing Brock for more than friendship or teen dating. There's a change in her. One I see in the eyes of other women. It boils my blood. I wish it were different with her. I wish I could feel less, like I do with every other aspect of my life. But it's like what I lack in emotion with everything else has forced me into feeling an overwhelming amount of adoration for her. Just her. My daughter, my blood, my miracle. Before her, I thought I was broken, born wrong. I'd never felt love until her finger wrapped around my thumb and her lungs let out the most perfect cry I'd ever heard.

Mine. Mine. Mine.

From her first breath, until her last.

I could pack our shit up and reinvent myself. I've done it before. But she wouldn't be willing, and that is where it would all crumble down. Keeping her away from those boys will mean killing Eric and his sons and fleeing this place with my precious daughter, but it's out of the question, so I need to learn to let this play out. Let her get her heart broken by the bastard who's too much like his father, then pick up the pieces.

She will always come home to me. I'm her daddy. Maybe now that she's getting ready for college, a move is in order. I could rent this place or just leave it closed up and empty. Buy something with no neighbors nearby.

I open my work emails and filter out the junk. It's been a while since I've been in the office putting in appearances. I make a note to do just that and schedule it around Lucy's life. I end up Googling Trevor Blackstone, because one can never know too much about their enemies, and roll my eyes when pictures of him and

Eric at corporate events flicker over the screen. Trevor appears to shy away from the cameras, whereas Eric lives for the limelight. His bought smile is wide in every shot. I power down the computer when I hear movement outside the kitchen window.

Grabbing a knife, I creep over and peek out. A half-naked female darts across the lawn, followed by Nixon giving chase. He catches her with ease and lifts her up and spins. She giggles, and he covers her mouth, shushing her. She wiggles from his hold, but doesn't flee. Instead, she turns to face him and bites her lip. He says something I can't make out and she shakes her head no. With a push on her shoulder, he directs her to her knees. She fiddles with his shorts, but it's obvious what's happening. I march toward the front door and open it silently.

Just as I step out onto the front step, I notice him reaching behind him for something tucked in the back of his shorts. A glint of silver catches the illumination of the street lights lining our properties.

"Nixon," I bark, my mind reeling with what I've just seen.

What would he have done if I hadn't come out?

He's only sixteen for fuck's sake.

Part of me wants to know so badly what he was about to do, but the other part knows I can't afford him spilling blood on my property.

Is he like me, just like I thought?

He doesn't startle and make a dash for it. He just looks over, staring me directly in the eye while the girl screeches and jumps to her feet before running back to the Pearson's house.

"What do you think you're doing?" I demand.

He doesn't answer me. Instead, he smiles before he darts off. It's so eerie, I question whether I made the whole scene up in my head.

Going back inside, I lock the front door, and for the first time since living here, I lock the back doors too.

FOUR FATHERS SERIES

EIGHT

JAX

Psychopath red flag
#9
They are impulsive

WORK IS EASY TO AVOID WHEN I HAVE LUCY to spend my time on. We went shopping together this morning. Though she didn't know I was with her, it was still special, seeing all the brands she likes. She invites eyes to look at her with the skimpy shorts she's always wearing, but I'm not complaining—not when she bends over to load up her car with groceries. The curve of her ass cheek is a work of art. I'm going to lick her there. There and everywhere. I follow behind her until she turns off to go toward Trevor's house. His car is there, so I continue on, deciding to do lunch at home and come back later when Trevor isn't around.

As soon as I enter the house, I notice Rowan's bag discarded on the foyer floor. I hate untidiness. It's lazy and unnecessary, and she knows it. I've been teaching her her entire life how to keep things neat and tidy.

"Sweetheart," I call out as I pick up her bag and place it on the hook before walking up the stairs to her room.

"I got done early. I thought we could—" My words fade to nothing and my world stops as Eric's obnoxious face looks back at me from Rowan's bedroom. *Her bedroom.*

The darkness inside me leaks into my bloodstream, powering me, taking over. I'm going to paint this room with his insides.

"Whoa, killer. Wipe the murderous glare off your face. I was here to help Rowan. She called, absolutely in tears with fear," he tells me, holding up his hands in surrender.

What the fuck? My rage retreats like a receding tide,

and in its place fear and worry overcome me.

"What's wrong? What happened?" I demand, searching behind him for my daughter's eyes.

Did Nixon scare her or try something? Would he hurt her?

"She thought it was an intruder," he tells me with a shrug, his voice smug. "Turns out, it was a mouse. I almost got the bastard, but he got away." He gestures to Rowan's dollhouse, the one I gave her for her birthday, which is now in pieces.

"I tried to stomp on his ass, but it didn't quite go as planned," he adds, and I want to crush his skull using just my palms. It's quite something feeling the crack of a skull under your grip. My eyes remain transfixed on what once resembled a dollhouse. "If you need help carrying that thing out of here, I'll send over one of the boys. Rowan is a woman now. She doesn't need to be playing with dollies."

What the hell did this ant say to me, in my home,

about my fucking daughter?

"Get the fuck out of my house, Pearson," I bark. The anger filters back in, demanding a price for his disrespect and overstepping.

"Daddy!" Rowan cries out almost in reprimand.

"What?!" we both snap at the same time.

Eric erupts in laughter, like it's the funniest shit he's ever done. How can anyone like this douchebag? He's, for lack of a better word, lame. He thinks he's a teenager, like one of his boys, and it's tragic.

"Sorry, I have kids too." He shrugs and pushes past me, nudging my shoulder as he leaves. It's not until he's gone that I want to question this entire story.

A fucking mouse in my house? Not a chance. I'm the only thing lurking around this house in the shadows.

Why would she call him? Why does she look guilty? Did she have one of his boys in here and he caught them and is covering for the little bastard? The red lipstick stains on his shirt no doubt came from my Rowan, and it pisses me off that he tried to console her with his sleazy hands as if he were her parent. He isn't, and I'll be damned if I let him ever be in her room again.

"Daddy?" Rowan questions meekly. It's then I realize I haven't moved and I'm still staring at the ruined dollhouse.

"Clear this mess up," I snap. "It will do for firewood."

Her mouth pops open in shock, but I've had enough for one day. I slam my bedroom door shut and pull off my clothes. I need a shower and a power nap. Right away, I notice someone's been in here and messed with my bed. I move over to the pillows and grab one, bringing it to my nose and inhaling.

Pussy.

Bile rises in my throat. I want to take a match to the room. Burn the whole fucking place down to nothing.

Rowan not only is sexually active with one of those little cunts next door, but disrespecting me in such a manner is beyond reasoning. Disappointment is a new feeling for me, but it crashes into me, leaving me discombobulated. I don't like the changes happening, or the distant feeling I'm having toward Rowan.

How has it come to this?

I have to spend more time with her. She's acting out because I haven't been giving her time like I used to. I dig out my phone and go on the internet to order a new bed, then shower away the images of my little girl being defiled in my own bed by one of the Pearson shitstains with the taps on scalding.

Rowan isn't at the table when I come down for breakfast. I hear voices from the window and make my way outside. Nixon's eyes flash toward me before he leans in, cradling Rowan's face and planting a deep kiss on her lips. I'd always assumed she was with Brock, so seeing her with Nixon surprises me. I move closer toward them, and refrain from plucking him by the balls and kicking the ever-living shit out of him. Rowan is eighteen, sure. A woman. Women kiss. And apparently, they do a lot fucking more in their daddy's bed.

So, it's Nixon she's with. I decide to allow it. If anything, I'm glad it's not Hayden out here with her. Although him fucking around with some girl the other night doesn't show loyalty to Rowan, and the whole knife aspect is alarming. If I tell Rowan about the girl he was messing around with, it will crush her and all this shit will be over. I'll console her, and things will go back to how they've always been.

I'm so caught up in my thoughts, I don't notice he's deepened the kiss and slips his hand down to her ass. Little asshole.

"What the fuck?" I snarl at him from behind her.

She immediately pulls away, and has the decency to blush and look guilty when she turns to see me standing there. "I-I just w-wanted to see him b-before school," she trips over her words, looking confused.

Nixon wraps his arms around her from behind, almost baiting me. He's more like his father than I thought. I sour at the realization. It's a shame.

"We're together," he announces, like he's telling me he's having an affair with my wife. If I had one, God forbid.

"Go home, boy," I snap. "I'm tired of the Pearson's crawling around my house like fucking cockroaches," I add, narrowing my eyes at him.

How many times must I warn these rodents before I can just do the world a favor and exterminate them?

Nixon doesn't even blink, my word ineffective. This is what I liked about Nixon; his indifference is so familiar, it was almost comforting to me, but not when he holds my daughter in his grip. I know the possessive touch of a boy—a man. I have one too, and it doesn't end well for the prey in my hold.

"See you soon, babe." He smirks.

Babe. Oh God, she's someone's babe. My daughter. How did I allow this to happen?

Her face is strained, like she wants to grin at him but

refrains.

She thinks this is amusing, her being groped on our doorstep by a dirty Pearson. She's forgotten she's one of many on a very long list of the Pearsons' walks of shame.

"In the house," I tell her, my tone leaving no room for argument. "You're grounded for a year," I add, and she scoffs.

"I love you, Daddy." She sighs, and it's such a small gesture. Three words, and I'm putty in her hands. I squeeze her to me, remembering the child I raised and not the floozy the boy next door is turning her into.

"I love you too, Rowan, but I'm serious about the Pearsons. I don't want you near any one of those little assholes. Especially Eric," I add on a whisper. He knows his son is corrupting her, and he no doubt thinks it's hilarious. Prick.

NINE

J A X

Psychopath red flag
#10
They need control

I HAVEN'T BEEN ABLE TO GIVE LUCY THE TIME I NEED to lock down the plans I have for her due to the fact that I've been trying to spend more time with Rowan. But now she's got herself a little babysitting job and is spending more time with her best friend who has the reddest hair I've ever seen. I have my time back, and my evenings are spent on Lucy.

I'm in Trevor's house, which she now lives in with him, but he leaves her alone a lot since Eric works him to the bone. Just like the night before, she's alone—perfect setup for me and my lovely to spend some quality time together. She's made herself at home here, covering every inch with her personality. Her scent. Her belongings. Her mess I find oddly endearing.

I spray her perfume into the room and ponder taking the bottle with me when I leave. The thought flees as quickly as it comes, and I place it back in its position on her dresser, then pick up her lotion, smearing a dot of the cream on my wrist.

I double check the tracker app I have on Trevor's car and let out a sigh of relief. He's still at Four Fathers, where he's been all day. That company will suck the rest of the years he has left on this planet in the blink of an eye. How anyone could choose to work late into the night when this beauty is at home waiting is beyond me.

The moonlight bleeds into the room, highlighting their bed like the moon is her own personal spotlight. I find myself drifting over to the bed and picking up her pillow, brushing my lips over it. It smells like the shampoo she uses, making my dick hard in my slacks. I'm wearing coveralls made for our pharmaceutical labs. They're uncomfortable and restrict my hands from rubbing over my cock. I make a rash decision to slip it off. I open the doors leading to her balcony and chuck the overalls down to the sand beneath. I'll collect them before I leave.

When I hear the front door open, I slide into her closet and wait.

Thud. Thud. Thud.

I'm so excited, my heart dances inside my ribcage. It doesn't take her long to get up to their room. It never does. She doesn't like lingering downstairs alone in this massive seaside home when Trevor's not here. Smart girl. She's tired, and it shows in her features. The music position at the school must be wearing her out. Or perhaps their relationship is on the rocks. Small, dark circles shade under her eyes, but she's still the most perfect thing I've seen.

The gap in the slats gives me enough of a view to watch as she strips out of her clothes, discarding them in a pile on the floor. Her tits are just as I imagined, round and perky, flushed nipples, hard and needy. Her tapered waist and curved hips are what music videos are inspired by. Her ass is fuller then I thought, and it only makes me more excited to claim her. My dick is impossibly hard as she disappears into the bathroom and turns on the shower. I wait for the shower door to close before I leave my hiding spot.

I know I should leave—get out while she's not in the room. I'm already pushing my luck and taking risks by exposing my skin, hair, and clothes inside this house, but she is different than the others.

I almost want to take her...*and keep her*.

I creep toward the open bathroom door, and before I know it, I'm inside.

The shower is steamed over the frosted glass separating us. I can see her form, though. She's facing away from me, humming as she strokes soap over her flesh.

My hand reaches out toward the glass, and I'm so fucking close, if she turns, she will know I'm here and it will be over.

I move backwards, stepping outside the bathroom, and pull my cock from my slacks. It's pulsating, throbbing painfully, the vein protruding and angry. Stroking firm, deep caresses from base to tip, I want to growl in relief. I stand just outside the door where I can still look at her. She bends to wash her feet, and her ass is prone. Her cunt would be in perfect view if not for the steam hiding it from me. I rub my cock harder and harder, the spray of the water pounding down on her, covering up my ragged breaths. I'm going to come. I can't prevent it. I need the release like I need my next breath, and the heat spreading up my spine warns me of its impending arrival.

I move back to her dresser and uncap her lotion container. I place it to my dick and give myself a final stroke. White spunk spurts into the lotion bottle, and I rush to finish, shoving my cock away and the lid back into place. I shake the bottle and place it down just as the shower turns off. I move back to the closet and wait. She takes a good five minutes in the bathroom before she emerges. She's wearing shorts and a tank top, and her hair is wet and combed back. My heart nearly bursts out of my chest when she walks over to her dresser and uncaps her lotion bottle, spreading the spurt of product mixed with my seed up her arm, over her shoulder, and down her chest. Her hand disappears inside her top and tents the fabric of her nightwear as she rubs the cream into her tits. Fuck, I'm instantly hard again. She's wearing me. I'm sinking into the pores of her skin. I think she knows, and she likes it.

She climbs into bed sighing, her eyes open. She lays awake, staring out at the moon for a while. Eventually, sleep claims her mind, while my cum claims her body.

Soon, my sweet Lucy.

I slip from the closet and out of the room. I'm out the house and collecting the coveralls within minutes.

So easy. So fucking perfect.

This is so unlike me, taking such risks, but I like the rush of it. I know it will become a routine.

TEN

J A X

Psychopath red flag
#**11**
You want them to like you

LUCY, LUCY, LUCY, TONIGHT IS THE NIGHT. NOT only will Trevor be at the office late, but I've punctured his tire, and it will take time to fix. We have all night together. She will learn the difference between a real man and a weasel. I'll never know what it is that keeps her with Trevor. Maybe it's the money.

Women are a mystery to me. Rowan refused to listen to me when I tried telling her about Nixon. I think I just pushed them closer together. Rowan's never home these days, and if I didn't have Lucy, it would eat me up that she's so out of control. I start the engine of my car and back into the space just behind some trees. As the headlights dim, a door opens on one of the houses and Eric Pearson emerges from inside. I smirk, wondering what poor whore he's brought here to one of Trevor's properties, but then the ground disappears and my mind scatters into pieces.

I'm literally being ripped apart inside as I try to compute what I'm seeing.

My Rowan.

And Eric. No. It can't be.

Would he be that fucking low?

I almost feel dumb for even thinking the question. Of course he would, and he also would want something his son had. He hates that they're young and just starting out in life. That he's getting older, his wife left him, and his sons despise him.

All my plans for Lucy flee for the moment. Ice water over a burning fire.

My baby girl is a whore for Eric fucking Pearson. I should have killed him months ago when I found him in our house.

Oh God, he was in our house. It wasn't his son she fucked in my bed. It was him. The proof was right in front of my goddamn face. He was standing in her bedroom for crying out loud.

How could I have overlooked this?

I'm going to have to take her away. I'll pack up, make arrangements, and we will leave. Then, when she's forgotten about that piece of shit and everyone has moved on, I'll slip back here and burn the house down with them all inside.

And I'll claim Lucy.

She's waited this long, she'll wait for me again.

My lovely is a good girl like that.

I place the gift I planned on injecting Lucy with back in the sunglasses case and lock the glove compartment with it inside. The fifteen-minute journey home takes eight minutes when breaking all speed limits. I pack Rowan a bag first. Just things I know she will want, like the fake photos of her mom, her teddy bear she keeps on her bed, and those old DVDs of *Hannah Montana* she used to love. She can watch them again and remember who she used to be.

Next is my stuff. I have to make sure I clear the basement and wipe all the computers in the house. I'll rent this place out eventually, or just let the fucking thing rot. I pack up the essentials from the house and move money around. I send an email to Lynn, my personal assistant who I interact with mostly by email, and inform her I won't be in the office for a while and to cancel any and all meetings for the near future. By the time I have everything in place, dawn is creeping over the horizon and Rowan still isn't home.

I wonder if Nixon is aware of Eric's betrayal. Exhaustion washes over me. My eyelids close without permission. Bloody but satisfying images of Nixon sitting on his father's chest as he carves him with his knife make me sleepy, and I drift off. Maybe I do like that kid.

It's afternoon when I jar awake. My hands tighten on the arms of the chair I fell asleep in. The bi-folding doors are open, and there's noise sounding from next door. I jump up and go to the patio. I hear Rowan's voice. Motherfucker. Storming over there, I push through the gate and see all the usual assholes together. And there's my fucking daughter right in the middle of them.

"Rowan," I bark. "Time to go home. Now." *And you'll never be coming back*, I add internally.

Everyone grows quiet, watching and waiting, expecting me to lose my shit. Within my mind, I've massacred them all in a hundred different scenarios, but Rowan is here. And so is Lucy, much to my surprise. She's with *him*, the sandal wearing prick. Damn, I was so close last night, I nearly claimed her.

Rowan stares warily in my direction from the pool. I don't want to show her my true self. Not ever. I still have hopes I can fix what this pervert has broken inside her.

Why would she let that filthy pig touch her?

He seduced her, tricked her, caught her when she'd no doubt been hurt by one of his cunt sons, and played on her emotions. I should have seen this happening, been there for her. Cut his cock off the day I found him in her room.

Eric smirks at me, a gloat evident in his eyes. This is a game to him. He's always been threatened by me and used a child as a way to get to me. I've never been interested in killing a child before, but to deliver his children to him one limb at a time is quite tempting right now.

"I just got here," Rowan says, pushing her lips out in a pout, her arms crossing over her chest, pushing her cleavage almost out of her top.

Nixon walks up behind her and wraps his arms around her, causing Eric to stiffen. This charade is so over. Nixon was in on this façade, protecting his daddy. Fucker. When Nixon decides to add to the show by kissing Rowan on her bare shoulder, I feel the impending storm building inside me.

They've ravished and ruined my baby. Turned her into a whore, just like her mother. The one thing that made me human is being stolen from me—my only grasp on normalcy, the one thing keeping me tethered to sanity is fading from my view.

"Rowan," I growl in warning.

"Out of the pool," Eric barks.

"Yes, Daddy," she murmurs, not to me, *to him*. To fucking Eric. She moves away from Nixon, offering him a pity smile, and takes the steps from the pool. She's on display for all eyes to see. And they all fucking look.

When did this happen?

When did I allow them to change her?

She grabs a towel and wraps it around her before coming to stand between us. I scan the scene before me, counting the bodies and deciding whether I could take them all. Eric is squaring off, trying to puff his chest out, thinking he could get the drop on me if things go south. He's delusional. I'd snap his neck so fast, no one would even realize he's dead before I'm on to the next one. I've already sought out items I'd use all around these dumb fucks. The fact that they wired speakers up and have them plugged into an outlet near the pool is a disaster waiting to happen. I could drop the live box into the pool and wipe the boys out in one clean sweep. The bottle Levi is drinking from is a perfect weapon to crack and burrow in his throat. So quick, so easy. Trevor would get the barbeque fork in the eye while my dick stiffened to Lucy's screams. She won't like the mayhem, but when it's all over, she will succumb and beg me to take her slow. And I will. I'll wrap my hands around her neck and mourn never being inside her as she fades from life under my grip. It's not how I wanted it to happen, but if the others have to go right now, she will too.

Rowan.

Fuck.

What have they done?

My eyes ignite with the images flashing through my mind, and Eric falters slightly, as if he can sense the monster before him. The one he's provoked and lured into his own backyard.

"Jax," Eric says, grinning like a shmuck, "you should stay and join us. Rowan is always telling us how lonely you are. So sad, man."

Rowan glares up at him. But she needn't worry about his pathetic attempts to mock me. I'm not lonely, quite the opposite. This is just a game to him. Well, games change, evolve, and the most important part he will learn soon enough is you can't win all games.

And he will not win this one.

"Rowan," I seethe, dragging her gaze back toward me. She hasn't moved, and my patience for her disobedience has reached its peak. "I don't know what the hell you've gotten yourself into over here, but you're done with these assholes."

"Dad," she pleads, her voice broken, just like her. Eric's crept inside her mind and polluted her. Eric saunters over to her, brazen. He's just put himself in my beast's jaw and I'm tightening my grip. I will eat this fucker alive. He just signed his death warrant. He places an arm around her in ownership and narrows his eyes on me over her head.

I've solidified; I can't move.

I've lost her.

She's not mine anymore.

He grabs her wrist in his overly tanned hand. "See this ring?" he goads me. "It means she's mine now."

Oh hell no you didn't.

"The fuck you say?" My voice is ice cold, deadly. He has an audience, so he's putting on a show. *Well, I won't jump just because you want me to.*

"Eric," Rowan whimpers. "Not like this. Not here," she pleads. But she's as delusional as he is if she thinks she has any power of him—over me. This was never a game she could win. She's just his pawn.

Ignoring her, he kisses the back of her hand while glaring at me. "She. Is. Mine," he tells me, holding out her hand like a severed limb. The diamond, too big for her petite finger, looks ridiculous and as obnoxious as him. "I put a ring on it."

"You fucking what?" I breathe, letting the rage fester in my chest, build and expand.

"I'm his fiancée," Rowan says proudly, lifting her chin and meeting my eyes. "And I'm pr..." she trails off as I take a menacing step toward her.

I don't see Rowan anymore.

I just see her mother.

A whore, laughing at me.

"You will regret the day you laid eyes on her," I tell Eric. My tone leaves no room for miscommunicating my promise. I will have my vengeance, and it will be swift and brutal. "I will end you, Eric Pearson."

"Get the fuck off my property." He grins. "My son will show you out," he adds as Nixon moves around them. "Try any shit and I'll end you first." Eric smirks. He has no idea his life is over. There's not enough money in the world that can save him from my wrath.

He reaches up and squeezes Rowan like she's a cheap slut he picked up and paid for from a street corner.

"Tell him, angel," he whispers into her ear. "Tell him how I already won."

She whimpers, but says the words just like he directs. Brainwashed. "I have a new daddy now."

Sickness roils in my belly like oil on a lake. Flames skate across that sickness, becoming a blazing inferno.

"And her new daddy takes really good care of her," he booms. "Really good care of her."

He's the kind of sick animal who should be put down at birth. His mother should have smothered the cocksucker while he was still in his crib.

The tricks he is so desperately trying to play with me just lost any power they once had. Rowan Wheeler is gone, and so is the Jaxson Wheeler I've tried so hard to be for her.

Father.

Friend.

Businessman.

I'm now just Wheeler.

~~**Father.**~~

~~**Friend.**~~

~~**Businessman.**~~

Killer.

ELEVEN

J A X

Psychopath red flag
#12
They don't scare

I EXIT THEIR BACKYARD WITH NIXON HOT ON MY heels. He doesn't say anything, and that's wise of him. I think he senses the emptiness inside me. Recognizes it. It intrigues him. I've never met another person like me before, and I've never wanted to. It's hard enough wading through the void inside myself and learning to tame the urges. Knowing someone else who's fighting the same battle and not having control over them would be frightening if I could feel fear. Control is something I seek and want, and everyone can be controlled if you really want to dissect their psyche and find the trigger inside them.

Everyone *but* me and people like me.

We're the superior beings not controlled by our emotions. Some people will say I'm acting out of emotion now. The love I've lost for Rowan. But it's not true— it's just that I refuse to lose to a man like Eric fucking Pearson. He wronged me on a level I can't ignore. I'm just not built that way.

"You okay with him taking what you want?" I ask Nixon. *What's fucking mine.*

He shrugs, and I want to laugh because I see it there in his eyes. The rage. I want to coax it out of him, send him spiraling into a murderous wrath, but Rowan's moans sound out into the air and my hands twitch. Nixon's face falls, and a cloud overcomes his features. Perhaps the affection for Rowan isn't faked on his part. When they get louder just inside the gate, bile forms in my throat, and Nixon storms off in the opposite direction of the house.

This ends today.

Eric Pearson ends today.

———

Grabbing the shovel from the basement, I get to work in the backyard. The sun is hot and blisters my skin, but I don't stop. I dig and dig. I've done this before.

Déjà vu, motherfucker.

Sweat coats every inch of my skin, and my mind focuses on turning this mud out until my shovel hits its goal.

The laughter and noise from next door soon falls silent, and the sun gives way to dark clouds. The sky opens up, pelting down droplets of rain. It crashes over my skin, soothing the blisters from the sunburn.

I can't believe it has come down to this. I never expected betrayal from Rowan, but she has her mother's blood coursing through her veins. I should have realized it was inevitable.

Thoughts of her mother filter into my mind.

She was my first kill. It was sloppy and impulsive. I'd met her in a bar. I was on a conference trip and staying at a hotel. I hated those events, but money gains you privilege in life, so establishing myself with wealth was always in my plan. I would then relocate to somewhere off the grid and enter the dark web to pay to have my fantasies fulfilled. I'd heard of an underground organization located in Russia where the more money you have, the darker your requests can be. I never planned on becoming what I am. But she forced my hand. I gave it all up for Rowan.

Her mother approached me that night and seduced me. I'd always been an awkward teen. Teased and mocked throughout high school. It took time for me to understand I was different. Better than them. I grew into my features, and my body formed nicely with exercise, but I'd never really test-drove my new appearance.

Until Rowan's mother.

She gave me all her attention, laughed at things I said,

and ignored every other person who approached her that night. She had picked me, and I liked that. I felt alive for the first time in my life. The idea of her pupils dilating under my throttling hands and her gasping for air as I cocooned her body beneath mine raced through my thoughts and heated my flesh. Toxins from the alcohol danced in my veins, and when she suggested we go to my room, I was buzzing with so many different needs, I almost ran to the room. She showed me things I'd only seen on porn sites. Her mouth touched every part of me. But when she climbed over me and lowered her body onto my cock, I felt so overpowered and conquered. I hated it. When I flipped her onto her back and smothered her mouth with my palm, a flood of adrenaline washed through me so powerful, I came on the spot. Red veins popped in her eyes and her chest slowed under mine. I knew she was dying. If I'd held on for just a couple more seconds, I knew she would perish. I pulled back, sighing as she inhaled air and then began laughing hysterically.

I climbed from the bed and backed up against the wall, shocked by her amusement.

"I had no idea you'd be a freaky one. Fuck, didn't think you'd let me up. I charge extra for you coming inside me by the way," she announced, smirking and shaking her head.

I felt like that school kid being mocked in the locker room. Overlooked by the popular girls. I couldn't move. She found my wallet and emptied it. Threw her clothes on and left me there. Her face haunted me for months afterwards, and then one day, while back in that town, I saw her leaving a gas station. It was fate. The hate and rage I'd built up over that time bubbled to the surface. I was moving without registering what was happening. Her back was to me, and all I had in my hand were my car keys. It was dark and barren. No one around. No one to witness. I fisted my keys, slipping my house key between my fingers, then I wrapped an arm around her chest and stabbed her in the neck. Hard jabs to puncture the skin.

The flesh on the neck is thin, and the artery is right there in offering. It was then I saw her bump. A baby growing inside her. All the power and rush I'd felt as the metal of my key broke her skin and the crimson river emptied from her neck drained from me. She was pregnant. My mind counted the months, and fate turned out to be a cruel cunt. I knew I had a small slither of time to get that child out of her before they both died. It was messy, and when I cut her stomach open in the back of my car and pulled a living being from her body, my world changed. I'd been rough, and the baby girl had a cut running across the top of her head. But it wasn't life threatening, and her hair would grow to cover that. I wrapped her in my jacket and drove the car to the salvage yard with Rowan in the passenger seat covered in her mother's blood.

The crusher destroyed the evidence for me. A name change, different location, and I was someone new. A father. My lust for the kill didn't wane, but I learned so much about myself because of Rowan's mother. And now it's come down to this.

Waltzing back inside the house, I open the safe and take out the gun I keep in there. I'm not a fan of guns. The noise is jarring and too easy, but for this occasion, it will do.

I make sure it's loaded and head next door. The front door is unlocked and the lights are on, but I don't encounter anyone downstairs. I don't venture upstairs where I hear the boys jeering and laughing at something playing on a television set.

One quick glance, and I locate Eric. I see him through the glass of the French doors leading onto his patio. Rowan is on his lap. I raise the gun and make my way out there. He startles when Rowan gasps and jumps up, holding her hands out.

"Daddy! What are you doing?" she shrieks, her voice wobbling.

I shake my head. "Look who's back to being Daddy,"

I mock, staring straight into the eyes of the man who's made my castle tumble down around me. I didn't think this would be the way I'd be caught—be the way Rowan learns who her Daddy really is.

"A bit over the top, Jaxson. Let's calm the fuck down and put the gun away," Eric attempts to placate, trying to keep his cool demeanor. But I see the fear flickering in his steely eyes. I can fucking smell it on him.

"Shut your mouth and move," I instruct, my tone cold and unyielding.

He gets up and holds his hands up in surrender, but laughs like I'm joking.

Does he not realize the danger he's toying with?

"Jax," he says, and I hear the plea in his use of the name I've been telling him to use for years.

Tears are streaming down Rowan's face, matching the rain dancing over the grounds around us. I must look as crazed as I feel, covered in mud and soaking wet, holding a gun.

Anyone else would see the danger before them, but Eric still thinks this is a game he can win. "My boys are all here," he hisses, anger quaking his voice. "Do you think you can get away with this?"

"Unless you want me to shoot your brains out here and then pay those boys a visit, I'd start fucking moving," I warn.

"Fine. Where are we going?" he demands, gritting his teeth. He keeps looking over at Rowan, who is shaking from head to toe.

"My yard."

"Daddy?" Rowan cries.

I glare at her, imploring for my love to return to me, to see the baby she once was, but she's been selfish and entitled. She cut out my hollow heart and destroyed it when she chose this loser over me.

"*He's* your daddy now, remember?" I tell her, expressionless. I jerk my hand with the gun in its grip, gesturing for Eric to start moving.

He begins walking, and I keep the gun aimed at the back of his head as I follow behind him. Rowan sniffles, pleading with a murmured, "Sorry. Please. I'm sorry."

It's too late for sorry, sweetheart.

"You've made your point, Jaxson," Eric growls, the rain saturating him. What a foolish fucking man he is. He really thinks I would allow this? His feet falter when they reach my back gate, but a hard shove, and he stumbles forward.

"What the fuck?" he bellows as the view of an open grave is laid out before him.

"Oh my God! Daddy! What is this? You've gone crazy!" Rowan screeches.

She's wrong. I haven't gone crazy. I've never thought so clearly in my entire life. There's no hesitation. I know what needs to happen, and what is going to happen. She will come face to face with the reality I've always kept hidden from her.

"I love him. I love him. I'm eighteen!" she screams,

like it makes a difference. She loves him. What a joke.

"Move," I bark as Eric slows, his feet slipping on the now wet mud. The rain isn't letting up, and neither am I.

"Is it because you don't have anyone? No one left to love you?" Rowan shrieks. And then laughter, just like her mother. "You have to let me grow up, Dad."

I ignore her, giving Eric all my attention. He's right on the cusp of toppling into the grave I created over six years ago. "What the...?" His words fail him. He turns to look at me, his eyes wide, water cascading down him, flattening his usually styled hair. He looks just like I've always seen him: a drowned rat.

"Who the hell is that?" he chokes, real emotion for once in his goddamn life in his voice.

"Someone you've been looking for. Say hello to your wife." I grin, and relish as the horror drains all the life from him before I pull the trigger. The crack pierces the air, followed by a blood-curdling scream from Rowan. Blood spatter hits me in the face, and washes away with the rain as Eric fucking Pearson's body collapses into the grave on top of the bones of his wife.

I win, motherfucker.

Rowan heaves and vomits. She's on her knees, shock ravishing her body and mind. "You killed him!" She lurches, looking down into the grave.

Screams echo through the night as she points down into the grave.

"Is that really Julia?" she sobs. "You killed his wife? Their mother?"

"I should have never cut you out of your mother," I spit.

Just as I'm about to turn and leave, Nixon comes barreling toward me, crashing into me. We both slip on the wet mud and fall to the ground. He lands a blow to my jaw, catching me off guard. It takes me a few seconds to recover and shove him off my body. He's weak compared to me, because he's only sixteen, but like me, he doesn't show fear. He's coming back at me, but freezes when I point the gun at him. I grin as I tease the trigger, but he bolts forward, smacking my hand, causing my finger to squeeze and the gun to fire off a round. We squabble for a few seconds, then I hit him across the nose with the butt of the gun, feeling it crunch under my blow. He stumbles back, bringing his hand up to survey the damage. Blood dribbles from his nose, and he smirks, the blood dripping into his mouth covering his white teeth. He looks crazed. It's then I notice Rowan laying on her back gasping for air, the rain coating her body in its punishing terrain.

A dark red patch spreads out across the material of her dress.

More Pearson boys rush into my yard, their gazes taking in the scene and rushing to Rowan. The bullet must have hit her. Our entire life together flickers like an old movie through my mind.

"Call a fucking ambulance. Stay with us, Rowan. Look at me." They all try to coach her at once.

"He killed us," she coughs, holding a hand to her

stomach. "He's killed our baby."

Baby? What the fuck does she mean?

"No," Brock snaps. "You're fine. It will be fine."

Baby? She's not pregnant. Fate wouldn't be that fucking cruel.

"An ambulance is coming. Hold on," Camden, the youngest Pearson, cries out.

I fade into the night. She belongs to them now. And I'm free to be who I am. No more hiding behind the title of Father. Jaxson Wheeler died this night alongside Eric Pearson. And a new man was born in his wake.

Nixon jumps up and gives chase. I find myself running until I'm clear from the house, and then I slow and turn to see him see coming for me. His feet are sluggish, and he glares at me. Black nothingness staring into me, seeking out the monster he knows.

"I don't want to kill you," I tell him honestly, still holding the gun I used on his father.

"You shot Rowan," he bellows. "She's your damn

daughter."

"She caught a stray bullet. I only wanted Eric."

"He's my father," he growls. "You think I won't avenge him?"

A smirk curls my lip. "You don't give a shit about him. And we both know he's not your father. Perhaps you should ask Uncle Trevor if he knows who your real daddy is."

A slight flinch alters his face, and it's the first time I've seen him affected by my words.

"If she dies, I'll come for you," he warns, and it's endearing in a fucked up sort of way.

"You love her?" I ask. The roads are quiet, and I wonder how long it will take for the ambulance to arrive.

"I feel things for her, but we both know we don't love anything."

And there it is. We are the same.

"Take care, Nixon. Don't make the mistakes I did," I urge him.

And then, I'm gone.

EPILOGUE ONE—

J A X

Psychopath red flag
#13
They're obsessive

SEEING MY NAME EMBLAZONED ON THE FRONT OF newspapers isn't as scary as I once assumed it would be. I like being famous. Well, my old self anyway. I'm someone new now.

I watch as she moves around her new house, room to room, tinkering and clearing up the mess her greying, old man boyfriend leaves behind. I've learned his schedules. The man is as meticulous as me when it comes to his routine, so I know exactly when he will and won't be home. Just like tonight. I know he's working late at the office. All this time, and Four Fathers is still picking up the pieces from the loss of their fearless leader.

I've bided my time and come back for her.

She was always waiting for me.

It'll make it all the much sweeter.

I slip the syringe from my sock and slide out of the coat closet. Quickly, I move against the far wall and wait for her to return to the kitchen. I've thought about nothing else the entire seven months I've kept my distance. Building a new life far away from this old one. I've changed my appearance and wonder if she'll recognize me straight away.

This drug I've brought here just for her takes hours to actually kill. I will have so much time with her to make up for the wait I've made us both suffer through. The old man won't come home until late, and by then, it'll be too late for him to save her.

Her feet shuffle toward where I'm waiting, and as soon as she's close enough, I step out, reaching for her and injecting her in the small freckle on her lower neck.

Her eyes widen, and she looks scared as she sways on her feet.

"It's okay, Lucy," I say, comforting her. She's no doubt been fed hate from Trevor about me. Killing Eric, his best friend, was bound to cause some friction, but Lucy should know what we have.

A few unsavory words won't change the solid bond between us.

Her body tumbles as the paralytic consumes her. I quickly grab her so she doesn't hurt herself with the fall. I lift her and carry her up to the room they share, placing her on the bed. I've fantasized about fucking her for longer than any of my other girls.

What we have is special and timeless.

I couldn't move on.

No one else caught my eye, and things felt unfinished. Lucy is mine. I needed to come back for her, claim her. I take my time stripping her, exposing her skin. Tears well in her bright eyes, and I kiss them away, relishing the burst of salty goodness exploding over my tongue. I know it's elation in her tears. She's been waiting as long as I have for this day.

My hands stroke over her body, reacquainting myself with her.

I missed you so much, lovely Lucy.

I've waited so long for you.

Pushing her legs apart, I see her cunt is seeping with need, and I sigh. This moment is beyond anything I could have imagined. Leaning down, I swipe my tongue over her slit, dipping through her folds and devouring her.

A phone shrills through the house, and I pause. The answering machine picks up after six rings. It beeps, and Nixon's voice speaks.

"Hey, Lucy. Rowan has gone into labor and wants you here."

Beep. Nothing.

My hand shakes, and I find myself taking a step away from the bed.

I knew Rowan had survived her gun shot. It was superficial; hit her hip bone and lodged itself into the joint. She walks with a slight limp, but nothing life changing.

I assumed the baby shit she was spewing was her mind losing the plot after everything she witnessed that night.

But she *is* having a baby.

My baby is having a baby.

The memories of me cutting her from her mother and hearing her first cry almost has my knees buckling.

My baby, having a baby. I made so many mistakes that led to the place we're at now. I thought all hope for ever feeling for Rowan, what I once had, vanished that night, but this overwhelming need to go to her has me abandoning Lucy.

"I'm sorry. I need to go," I inform her, my lips still wet from her sweet cunt. She and I just weren't meant to be, it would seem. After all this longing and waiting, she will die hopeless and alone.

I'm sorry, Lucy.

I rush from the property and jump in the car I'm using while in town. I put a hat on when I reach the hospital and bring up the layout on the app I downloaded onto my phone. It's amazing what you can do with apps. There's a fucking app for everything these days, making life for wanted criminals easier to go undetected.

I avoid all the busy parts of the hospital and locate the laundry room.

"Sir, you can't be in here," a woman tells me, shaking her head and pointing to the door. I don't have time to come up with something witty to win her over. Instead, I rush her, gripping her head in my palms and twisting violently until her neck pops with a snap.

I toss her over my shoulder and drop her in one of the large carts full of soiled fabrics.

Locking the door, I strip from my clothes and stuff them in the trash, locating a surgeon's outfit to fit me. I dress the part, and slip from the room. Keeping my eyes down and surgical mask in place, I stay out of the way of other doctors until I'm where I need to be.

I slip behind the desk of the labor ward and look up the patients on the computer.

"Do you need help, Doctor?" a young woman in scrubs asks.

"No." I don't look up at her. Instead, I carry on searching until I find Rowan.

Delivered.

I jump up and move to the nursery.

My heart is in my throat. I thought this feeling had left me forever, but the anticipation is overwhelming. I reach the newborn room and look through the glass at all the new life, fresh and wrapped in blankets. Cries echo in the air. Then, I see her.

The name tag. "Wheeler."

All the emotion I felt for Rowan hits me once more. Mine.

—EPILOGUE TWO

R O W A N

Psychopath red flag
#14
They take what they believe to be theirs

P AIN, SHARP AND CONSTANT, ANNOYS ME FROM MY
hip. I've just had a baby cut from my womb not
four hours ago, yet it's the stupid hip that's giving me
problems.

This day should be so different, but here I am, a single
mother with no real family.

Eric's sons have taken care of me, but it doesn't end
the weird hollow hole I feel inside me since losing their
father and mine. I want to hate my dad for what he did,
and I do, but it doesn't erase the love I still feel for him.
It's such a weird thing to feel. Hate and love in equal

measure. I don't know where my dad is, or if he'll ever come back for me, or what I'd do if he did—or what the Pearson boys would do.

They want blood.

Blood for blood.

I try not to think about those things when I'm with them.

Hayden has taken the reigns and morphed into a man overnight. He's had to. He became heir to an empire. Trevor, Mateo, and Levi have welcomed him into the fold, desperate for a Pearson to hold their entire world together. And Hayden didn't disappoint. He's a lot like his father.

I look at my cell phone and frown. Still nothing from Lucy. She promised she'd be here for the birth of my baby girl, but she didn't make it, and she hasn't visited since. I text Trevor to ask if he's heard from her, but ten minutes pass, and he still doesn't reply.

Life is going to be so different for me. No college. I'm

a mother.

A mother. God, she's a miracle baby, and her brothers are determined to be a part of every aspect of her upbringing. I can't deny them. I love them and want to be around them. Even if it causes friction between the brothers.

The room door barges open, startling me, and Nixon fills the space. He looks wild, his eyes wide and jaw tense.

I sit up, nerves eating away at my stomach. "What is it?" I ask, breathless.

"Lucy. Trevor found her drugged and naked at her house."

The room expands, then closes in around me. "What?"

"She's here in the hospital. They're trying to determine what's in her system, but she's still alive."

Camden and Brock push into the room past Nixon. They look pale and shaken.

"She will be okay," I comfort them, but really, it's to

comfort myself. We can't lose anyone else. I can't. What the hell happened?

"Row, that's not all," Nixon says in a tone I've never heard him use before. It's almost fear. Camden moves to the bed and takes my hand, squeezing it.

"What? What is it?" I plead, terror beginning to eat its way up my throat.

"The baby. She's gone."

"The baby. She's gone."

"The baby. She's gone."

The words roll around my mind like a carousel. My body moves to stand, but my legs aren't working. I fumble and drop to the floor. All three of the boys surround me, but I can't focus.

"Where's my baby?" I shout.

I think of her steely blue eyes identical to her father's, and a sob clogs my throat.

"Rowan, we will get her back," Brock vows, staring so intently at me, I swear it's Eric incarnate.

"Where's my baby?" I screech.

"We think your father has taken her," Nixon states.

What? No. No.

I'm losing my touch on reality. Darkness clouds around me, and I drown in the ache, the pain of knowing he's taken her to punish me.

To start over.

To have someone who loves him.

She's gone.

She's gone.

She's gone...

The END!

COMING SOON

FOUR AUTHORS

FOUR GENRES

FOUR STORIES

<u>FOUR SONS</u>

ENJOYED THIS BOOK?
MEET THE OTHER FATHERS

Four Fathers Series by bestselling authors

J.D. Hollyfield, Dani René,

K Webster, and Ker Dukey

Four genres.

Four bestselling authors.

Four different stories.

Four weeks in April.

One intense, sexy,

thrilling ride from beginning to end!

***These books were designed so you can read them out of

order. However, they each interconnect and would be best

enjoyed by reading them all!***

She's not into him.
He doesn't care.

BLACKSTONE

A FOUR FATHERS STORY

J.D. HOLLYFIELD

OTHER BOOKS IN THE
FOUR FATHERS SERIES

BLACKSTONE
BY J.D. HOLLYFIELD

Contemporary Romance

I am meticulous. Structured. A single father.
I obsess over things and crave control.
And when a hot, feisty little woman throws a wrench in
my carefully laid out plans, I lose my mind.
My every thought revolves around making her bend to
my will—until they become less about her doing things
my way and more about just her.
My name is Trevor Blackstone.
I am an obsessive, complicated, demanding man.
People may not understand me, but it doesn't stop them
from wanting me.

KINGSTON

A FOUR FATHERS STORY

She works for him.
He doesn't care.

DANI RENÉ

OTHER BOOKS IN THE
FOUR FATHERS SERIES

KINGSTON
BY DANI RENÉ

Erotic Romance

I am arrogant. Insatiable. A single father.
I desire things that would make most people blush.
Normally, I find outlets that allow me to free the sexual
beast living within and play to my heart's content.
And when my voluptuous, innocent assistant starts
starving me after a little taste, I decide I'll let my inner
animal feed—on her.
Trouble is, once I have her, I can't let her go, and that
makes things complicated.
My name is Levi Kingston.
I am a dirty, ravenous, greedy man.
People may detest my kinks, but it doesn't stop them
from wanting me.

PEARSON

A FOUR FATHERS STORY

She's too young for him.
He doesn't care.

K WEBSTER

OTHER BOOKS IN THE
FOUR FATHERS SERIES

PEARSON
BY K WEBSTER

Taboo Romance

I am selfish. Spoiled. A single father.
I do what I want because I can.
One of my four sons is dating the hot,
young little neighbor...
Too bad it won't last long.
When I want something, I take it—even if it means
taking from my son.
My name is Eric Pearson.
I am an unapologetic, egotistical, domineering man.
People may not like me, but it doesn't stop them from
wanting me.

OTHER BOOKS

The Empathy series

Empathy

Desolate

Vacant

Deadly

The Deception series: -

Co-written with D.H Sidebottom.

FaCade

Cadence

Beneath Innocence - Novella

The Lilith's Amy MC series.

Co-written with D.H Sidebottom.

Taking Avery

Finding Rhiannon

Coming Home – Coming soon

The Broken Series:

The Broken

The Broken Parts Of Us

The Broken Tethers That Bind Us – Novella

The Broken Forever – Novella

The Men By Numbers Series

Ten

Six

Lucky No7 - RTBA

Drawn to you series

Drawn to you

Lines Drawn

Standalone novels:

My soul Keeper

Lost

I see you

The Beats In Rift

Devil

The Pretty Little dolls series:

Co-written with K Webster.

Pretty Stolen Dolls

Pretty Lost Dolls

Pretty New Doll

Pretty Broken Dolls

The V Games Series.

Co-written with K Webster.

Vlad. Out now.

Ven – Coming soon

ACKNOWLEDGMENTS

Thank you to you the reader for joining us on this new journey. Four Father's was an exciting project and something different for me to be involved in. I loved these assholes and I hope you did too. You've always got my back and follow me blind down any rabbit hole I push you toward. Thank you for your love, trust, and passion.

__Kristi,__ As always, it's a pleasure working with you. Although we didn't co-write this time your eyes and tweaking of my awful formatting and grammar errors are much appreciated. I adore working with you and love you, lady.

__Dani,__ Thank you for your beautiful formatting work. It's been fun working with you and getting to know your style and characters. I'm grateful for gaining two new friends from this project.

Jessica, Thank you for letting me share your character and stalk the shit out of her. It's been so much fun working on these together and I'm looking forward to K, birthing more projects for us to throw our creativity into.

My family always sacrifice time with me so I can work on creating book babies, thank you for being patient, eating takeout when I'm too tired to cook for you. For wearing creased clothes because Ironing is a waste of life hours and for putting up with me wearing headphones for 80% of the day and making you repeat what you tell me at least three times before I listen.

These titles don't happen with just us so **THANK YOU** to all the below:

Editor: Monica, thanks for joining us for another thrilling journey, we value your advice and your awesome skills. These badass daddies just wouldn't be as badass without your input.

Formatter: Dani, thank you for working your magic, they're beautiful.

Proof/Arc readers: Teresa, thank you for your keen eye, you're amazing.

Bloggers. We adore you for all your passion, time and help with sharing, reading and getting our work out there. Without you, we're floating on a sinking ship in a bottomless sea. Your love, loyalty, and trust know no bounds. You're our rock stars. Thank you.

Authors/friends: Thank you for sharing and caring. For knowing there's room for us all and for boosting each other up in these shark invested waters of late.

My group: (Dukey's darker souls) Thank you to my wonderful admin and incredible readers, cheerleaders, nosey parkers and slutty members. You guys are the highlight of each release. Your enthusiasm it beyond anything I could ask for. I know when you're nagging me for more it's a compliment so keep on pushing me and I'll keep on providing.

PA: Terrie, thank you for always having my back and being there to pick up the slack if I need to take a moment. You've always been my friend before my PA and I love you.

Kirsty Moseley,

You are my daily lifeline, when I need someone you're always there for me. Thank you for being such a great friend to me. For inspiring me, always boosting my confidence in my ability and sharing all the things you learn along the way. Every girl needs a Kirsty Moseley in their corner but they can't have you, because you're mine!! (Insert evil laugh)

ABOUT KER

My books all tend to be darker romance, edge of your seat, angst-filled reads. My advice to my readers when starting one of my titles... prepare for the unexpected.

I have always had a passion for storytelling, whether it be through lyrics or bedtime stories with my sisters growing up.

My mom would always have a book in her hand when I was young and passed on her love for reading, inspiring me to venture into writing my own. Not all love stories are made from light; some are created in darkness but are just as powerful and worth telling.

When I'm not lost in the world of characters, I love spending time with my family. I'm a mom and that comes first in my life, but when I do get down time, I love attending music concerts or reading events with my younger sister.

STALK LINKS

News Letter sign up
http://eepurl.com/OpJxT

Amazon Author Page
https://www.amazon.com/Ker-Dukey

Website
http://authorkerdukey.com

Facebook
https://www.facebook.com/KerDukeyauthor

Twitter
https://twitter.com/KerDukeyauthor

Contact me here
Ker: Kerryduke34@gmail.com
Ker's PA: terriesin@gmail.com

Made in the USA
Lexington, KY
13 September 2019